Dear Reader,

Looking back over the years, I find it hard to realise that twenty-six of them have gone by since I wrote my first book—*Sister Peters in Amsterdam*. It wasn't until I started writing about her that I found that once I had started writing, nothing was going to make me stop —and at that time I had no intention of sending it to a publisher. It was my daughter who urged me to try my luck.

I shall never forget the thrill of having my first book accepted. A thrill I still get each time a new story is accepted. Writing to me is such a pleasure, and seeing a story unfolding on my old typewriter is like watching a film and wondering how it will end. Happily of course.

To have so many of my books re-published is such a delightful thing to happen and I can only hope that those who read them will share my pleasure in seeing them on the bookshelves again. . .and enjoy reading them.

Back by Popular Demand

A collector's edition of forty favourite titles from one of the world's best-loved romance authors. Mills & Boon are proud to bring back these sought after titles and present them as one cherished collection.

BETTY NEELS: COLLECTOR'S EDITION

THE SILVER THAW

BY
BETTY NEELS

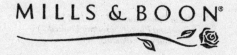

MILLS & BOON®

First published in Great Britain 1980 by Mills & Boon Limited
This edition 1997
Harlequin Mills & Boon Limited,
Eton House, 18-24 Paradise Road, Richmond, Surrey, TW9 1SR

© Betty Neels 1980

ISBN 0 263 79899 2

Set in Times Roman 12 on 12.5 pt by
Rowland Phototypesetting Limited
Bury St Edmunds, Suffolk

73-9701-46290

Printed and bound in Great Britain
by BPC Paperbacks Limited, Aylesbury

CHAPTER ONE

THE operating theatre was quiet; not a peaceful quiet, though. Mr Thomley-Jones was in a bad temper and although he was working with his usual meticulous care and skill, he was making life hard for those in attendance upon him, snapping and snarling his way through a cholescystectomy, two nasty appendices —both pushed in between the other cases because they could have perforated at any moment —and now with a still nastier splenectomy almost completed, he was venting his wrath on the hapless house surgeon who was assisting himself and his registrar. The unfortunate young man, clumsy in any case, became even more so, dropping things, tightening retractors when they should have been loosened, using the wrong scissors and generally making a fine muddle. His chief waited in mounting impatience and a silence which spoke for itself while his assistant cut the ends of gut with which Mr Thomley-Jones was reassembling his patient's inside and then let out a great roar as the unfortunate young man cut too close so that the stitch was no longer a stitch The registrar sighed soundlessly and

5

took over, the thunder of his chief's rage leaving him unmoved.

Just as unmoved was Mr Thomley-Jones' theatre Sister, who in one swift movement removed the scissors from the hapless surgeon's hand, gave him a swab to hold, handed more gut to Mr Thomley-Jones, threaded another needle ready for the mattress stitches and swept her gaze round the theatre. The theatre mechanic was standing stolidly by the anaesthetist, her staff nurse was checking swabs, the more senior of the student nurses was looking frightened but doing just as she should, and her companion, fresh in the theatre that very morning, was in tears.

She put the needle and gut into Mr Thomley-Jones' impatient hand and said in a quelling voice: 'Sir, you've made one of my nurses cry.'

'Bah!' exclaimed Mr Thomley-Jones, 'she shouldn't be in theatre if she's got no guts for it.'

Theatre Sister looked at him from a pair of fine dark eyes, heavily lashed. 'Unlike many of the people who come here, she has got guts, but when you get annoyed you're rather awesome, sir.'

He glanced at her and although she couldn't see his face she knew that he was pleased at being called awesome—it sounded godlike.

'Impertinent young woman, aren't you, Sister?'

'I'm sorry if you think so, sir, but I try to look after my nurses.'

He held out a hand for more gut and she inserted it into the needle-holder with great neatness.

'Oh, you do that all right, teach 'em well, too. You're a good one at your job, Amelia.'

When he called her by her name she knew that she had been forgiven. They had worked together now for four years and had a proper respect for each other's job; as the operation drew to its close he mellowed visibly so that the houseman was emboldened to take up the scissors again and the registrar winked at Amelia.

The surgeons went away presently to drink their coffee in her little office down the corridor, and, the patient safely despatched to his ward, the anaesthetist wandered away to join his colleagues, leaving the mechanic to tidy up after him while Amelia collected her nurses and set about the task of clearing away and setting up for the afternoon list. But presently she left Sybil, her staff nurse, and the student nurse and guided her new member of the team into the anaesthetic room where she was at pains to explain to the still tearful girl that Mr Thomley-Jones' bark was a great deal worse than his bite, that in time she would find that she could continue with her tasks in theatre whatever happened and that she had done very well for her first morning. 'And just you remember,' said Amelia soothingly, jumping down from the trolley where she had perched herself, 'one day you'll probably be a theatre Sister yourself. It's a splendid job, you know.'

With which heartening words she took herself off to join the gentlemen; they liked her to be there while they relaxed after a list, to pour their coffee and hand them biscuits and make an attentive audience of one while they chewed over their work. It was a nice job, she mused, going down the corridor, but after four years she was beginning to wonder if she wanted it for much longer; she was twenty-seven now, almost twenty-eight and although she had been engaged for a year to Tom Crouch, the Medical Registrar, he had made it evident that he expected her to go on working for some years after they were married, and as his reasons were sound and sensible she had stifled her disappointment and agreed to stay at St Ansell's. Tom was clever and doing well and he wanted to do better. He was anxious to make a success of his life and give her the things he considered that she should have; he was quite stubborn about this, and it was a pity, for she was the only daughter of a very comfortably placed village squire, able to provide all the comforts and luxuries Tom wanted her to have as well as helping him up the ladder. It seemed a waste of time to go on working while he saved enough to buy himself into a practice when she could have married him at once and enjoyed all the pleasure of running her own home. She saw his point of view, of course, but sometimes when she was tired at the end of a long day, she wondered if he weren't being selfish—well, not selfish, just a bit thoughtless. . .

There was almost no coffee left; she went in search of more, was scolded by the theatre maid and returned to pour second cups and the remainder for herself. She drank it fairly quickly and then excused herself and went back to the theatre, thankful that it was one of the days when only one theatre was in use.

The afternoon list, with Mr Godwin operating, went peacefully. He was a small, good-natured man, not in the least temperamental, and a good surgeon. But he was slow; by five o'clock Amelia was tired and a little cross. Thank heaven, she thought, Tom was free and they would go out to dinner somewhere quiet, and in two days she would go home for her days off. The thought got her through the rest of the afternoon and presently she was curled up on the rather shabby sofa in the Sisters' sitting room, drinking the teapot dry and contemplating her evening.

Tom had said seven o'clock, and well before that time she climbed the stairs to her room, had a bath and got changed, and because she had the time to spare she took extra trouble with her face and hair. The result was satisfactory even to her critical eye; her hair, a rich deep brown, she had brushed smooth into a chignon, her pretty face, with its delicately tilted nose and wide curved mouth, she had made up with care and her dress, a lacy knit jersey in a lovely rich ochre, although plain and very simple, had the simplicity of good cut and material. It suited her tall well-built figure to perfection and for once she found no reason to moan over her shape, which while it left nothing to be desired, was on the Junoesque side.

She was still a little early, but she put on an angora coat against the September chill and went downstairs.

Tom wasn't there, but she hadn't expected him to be. She whiled away ten minutes or so talking to Giles, the Head Porter, and then turned at Tom's quiet: 'Sorry to keep you waiting, Amelia.'

She beamed up at him, wishing secretly that old Giles or no, he would kiss her or at least take her hand—after all, they had been engaged for some time now and there was nothing secret about it. She stifled regret and told herself that Tom always did the right thing and whereas she was impulsive and inclined to want her own way, he was invariably correct in his behaviour and deliberate in his decisions. She went out to his well-kept Rover and got in beside him, and he drove, with all due regard for the Rules of the Road, into the stream of evening traffic.

They almost always went to the same restaurant, an Italian one in the Brompton Road, and the head waiter showed them to their usual table with a welcoming smile. As they sat down Tom observed: 'That's a new dress, isn't it, Amelia?'

'Yes—do you like it?'

'Very much—I suppose it cost a month's salary?' He smiled at her as he spoke, but it was a thin smile, and she sighed a little when she saw it.

'It was expensive, Tom—I like clothes, most women do, but I'd cheerfully wear the same old thing for years if it would help you—but you won't be helped. . .'

'No. Will you mind after we're married, not being able to buy anything you take a fancy to?'

She felt surprise. 'But Tom, you won't mind me spending my own money, will you? You know I've got an allowance, and it isn't just one Father gives me, you know—it's from some money my mother left to me. It doesn't matter what I do, it'll be paid to me for as long as I live.'

Tom was studying the menu. 'When we marry, it will be when I can support you fittingly as my wife, my dear   you will have an allowance from me.'

She gave him a bewildered look. 'But if I'm still working. . .?'

'That's a different matter. We shall both be earning and saving for our future.'

She couldn't see the difference herself, but she didn't say any more. It was very likely that being an only child of a loving although somewhat carefree parent, she had been spoilt and indulged and had grown up with all the wrong ideas. She studied the menu and made a mental resolve not to wear a new dress for a long time.

She went home two days later, to the small village in the Cotswolds where she had been born and had spent her childhood. Her mother had been alive then; it was only when she had died that Amelia had been sent away to a well-known girls' boarding school and when she had left there she had refused point blank to go to the finishing school to which her father had been advised to send her, but had stayed at home, running the rambling old house, riding Sorrel, the elderly mare, learning how to be a good housewife from Bonny the housekeeper who had been there ever since she could remember.

The realisation that she wanted to do something more than these things came slowly and helping to nurse her father through a bad attack of pneumonia decided her. She enrolled as a student nurse at St Ansell's, passed her exams brilliantly and at the age of twenty-four found herself theatre Sister in charge of the two main theatres in the hospital. She had met Tom a year later and the following year they had got engaged. She had taken him home to meet her father and proudly displayed the solitaire diamond ring he had given her. It was a small diamond but a good one; Tom never bought rubbish.

Her father met her at the station and drove her the several miles home. Amelia had a little car of her own, but she had left it behind on her last leave to have it serviced at the local garage; now she would be able to drive herself back. She sat happily beside her father and looked around her. The country was beautiful, it always was, but autumn was her time of year; she loved the colours and the smell of bonfires and the trees turning from green to gold and brown and red. She was only half listening to her father telling her about the trout he had almost caught, the new fly he had made, the old pike which still evaded even the most beguiling bait—he was an enthusiastic fisherman and ever since her mother died she had accompanied him on several trips. She didn't like fishing herself, but over the years she had learnt a good deal about it. She turned to look at her parent now, smiling a little. He was a big man, stooping a little now, with a fine head of white hair and a luxurious moustache which didn't conceal the good looks which she had inherited, although it was her mother's dark eyes which enhanced them. They twinkled nicely now.

'You sound thoroughly put out with the fishing, Father—why not try Scotland for a week or two?'

He gave a rich chuckle and swung the old Bentley through the open gate and up the drive to the lovely old house at its end. 'Better than that, my dear. I thought I might try Norway—old Jenks is just back; had a splendid time—can't remember the place, but there was more fish than he could take. Why don't you come with me? We'll hire a boat and you can see to the food and so on.'

They were crossing the gravel to the house, but she stopped and looked at him with faint horror. 'But Father, it's September—the end of September, it'll be cold. . .'

'Pooh, what's a chilly wind or so? Why not get Tom to come along too?'

'Tom? Well, yes, he's got a week's leave due—but I've got three. . .'

'Well, he can come for a week, can't he? It's only a short flight from Heathrow.' He stumped across the wide panelled hall. 'Give you a chance to talk—getting married and so on. Haven't you got a date fixed yet?'

Bonny, the housekeeper, had appeared to open the drawing room door and tell them that lunch would be half an hour and it looked, if she might be so bold as to say so, as if Miss Amelia needed a few good meals.

Amelia gave her a hug, assured her that she never felt better but would undertake to eat anything she had cooked and went to sit by the wood fire burning in the stone fireplace. When Bonny had gone she said:

'Tom wants to get a bit more money saved— we thought in about two years' time, and I'll go on working.' She sounded a bit defiant, and her father didn't say anything for a minute but poured their sherry with care.

'Well, you're old enough to know your own minds,' he said gruffly. 'Most young people seem to set up house together without a thought of the future, nor for that matter, of getting married—that seems to come later.'

'Tom isn't like that.'

Mr Crosbie looked as though he was going to say something, changed his mind and handed her the glass instead. 'Anyway,' he said mildly, 'a week's holiday can't interfere with your plans, can it, and I don't suppose Tom will object to you staying on another couple of weeks with me. He's a reasonable man.'

Amelia relieved at getting the bit about them not marrying for a bit off her chest, conceded that he wouldn't mind at all and three weeks would be fun. 'When were you thinking of going?' she asked.

'It's—let me see—the twentieth today.

Could you manage ten days from now?'

She frowned. 'Yes, I expect so. Mr
Thomley-Jones is going on holiday, which
will cut the lists quite a bit, and Mary Symes,
who does the relieving, comes off Women's
Surgical in a week's time—she could take
over. I'll see what I can do.'

Her father nodded. 'Good—try and
arrange something and fix it with Tom if you
can, my dear.'

They lunched together in the rather dark,
oak-panelled dining room with Badger, who
had been with the family for most of his life,
waiting on them in a rather absent-minded
fashion. They discussed the coming trip,
arguing the advantages of flying to Bergen
or taking the car over from Newcastle.

'We'll fly,' decided Mr Crosbie. 'We can
rent a car over there—I've the address of
someone we can get a boat from and a list of
hotels from Jenks.' He shot Amelia a look.
'No dressing up, mind you,' he warned, 'and
take warm clothing. There's a small place,
Stokmarknes, where he says there's quite
a good hotel, and if we want a change
there's Harstad. There's a road,' he added
laconically.

'I should hope so—will it be very
isolated?'

'Not where we're going,' he reassured her,
'and we shall be on the Coastal Route, the
ships call most days and it's only an hour or

so from one place to the next. If you get bored you can go off for the day, you and Tom.'

It might be a good idea, Amelia thought, to have Tom to herself, miles away from his work and the hospital, and try and get him to change his mind about their future. 'It sounds super. I'll talk to him as soon as I get back.'

She spent her two days riding, grooming the two elderly donkeys who kept her own horse and her father's great skewbald company, pottering about the garden, listening to Job, the old gardener, carrying on about his rheumatism, the apple crop and the incredible size of his pumpkins. And when he told her, with the familiarity of an old and trusted servant, to let him get on with his work, she wandered indoors to the kitchen and sat on the kitchen table while Bonny got the lunch, gobbling up biscuits from the tin Bonny had just filled.

'You'll get fat,' said Bonny.

'I haven't gained an ounce in two years,' Amelia told her happily, 'I work too hard.' All the same she got down and crossed to where an old-fashioned mirror hung against a wall and studied what she could see of her person. She wasn't conceited, but it gave her no misgivings. True, she was a bit too curvy for modern fashion, but she was a big girl and if she had been thinner she would stand in danger of looking like a clothes pole. 'I won't eat any more biscuits before lunch,' she observed, and took an apple from the dish on the kitchen table as she went out.

She saw Tom when she returned to St Ansell's; he had come into theatre to pass on a report about one of his patients, due for surgery the following day. The list was over and Amelia, in her office dealing with the paper work, looked up smiling as he went in.

He didn't kiss her, even though there wasn't anyone around to see; he had pointed out gravely when they had first become engaged that he didn't mix work with his private life, and they were both on duty, and she had accepted that although she hadn't agreed with him entirely. He smiled back at her now and asked: 'Busy?'

'Not really—just finishing off the bits and pieces. Tom, can you get a week's leave?'

He was reading up some case notes, but he put them down again to look at her. 'Yes, I think so—why?'

Amelia explained about the fishing trip and went on: 'It seemed a good idea—we don't see all that much of each other: we could have a week's peace and quiet—we'll have to see something of father, of course. . .'

He looked surprised. 'Well, of course; I don't know much about fishing, but I'm sure I shall enjoy trying my hand at it, but isn't it a bit late in the year for that part of the world?'

'Well, Father doesn't seem to think so — it'll be chilly, and dark in the evenings, I suppose, but he says the hotel is quite comfortable. He suggested that we could go off for local trips if we wanted. . .'

'Oh, I don't suppose we'll want to do that,' said Tom easily, and didn't see the little gleam of temper in her eyes. 'I mean, a week isn't very long, is it? You can go off sightseeing when you're on your own.'

She stifled a wish to tell him that she didn't want to go anywhere on her own, only with him; their times together were nearly always bound by the need to get back on duty and if they went away they would have every day in which to do exactly what they wanted. 'Yes, of course,' she agreed quietly.

She went home again on her next days off, this time driving herself in the Mini, to find her father deep in preparations for the trip, his whole interest concentrated on fishing rods, hooks, bait and all the paraphernalia of the dedicated fisherman, so Amelia spent a morning with Badger, packing a case with the right sort of clothes for her father, and then went away to her own room to render herself the same service.

It was a lovely day, clear and blue-skied and sunny, and if it hadn't been for the leaves all over the lawns and the trees changing their colours she might have supposed it was summer. She went and sat on the window seat and looked out on to the flower beds below, watching Job carefully taking off the dead roses. It was his boast, and no one had disputed it, that he could pick roses until Christmas; he certainly took great care of them. She got up presently and went to her clothes closet and began to look through it; no dressing up, her father had said. She chose two pairs of cord slacks, some thick sweaters and a quilted jacket with a hood and a pair of wellingtons, thick gloves too and a couple of scarves, and then because there might be a tiny chance of wearing something else, she added a pleated skirt and matching bolero and two blouses to go with them and as an afterthought a jersey dress in a warm burgundy. She found a pair of shoes, some tough ankle boots she wore when she went walking, and packed them into her Gucci case, filling in the corners with undies and night clothes and stockings. She would be coming on holiday in a few days, but it seemed a good idea to be packed and ready before then—there wouldn't be much time. They were to travel on a morning flight to Bergen and she wouldn't be able to get home before late evening before that. She put the case tidily in the closet and went downstairs to find her father.

She had only four days to do before she went on holiday, but they were busy; Mr Thomley-Jones, due to go the day before her, had suddenly become determined to do twice as many cases as he usually did, which left them all stretched to their limit. Fortunately, the new student nurse, after her first disastrous day, was shaping very well, and Nurse Knollys, who had been off sick for several weeks, was back again. A large, ungainly girl with no looks to speak of, she was utterly dependable in theatre. Amelia, wishing her nurses a cheerful good morning on the last day before her holiday, sighed thankfully that all her staff were there. Sybil could be relied upon to keep them all up to scratch, and Mary Symes would be able to cope—Mr Thomley-Jones wouldn't be there and the other four surgeons who operated were calm, quiet men who seldom raised their voices. . .

She went to scrub presently. The morning's list was a long one and there were a couple of laparotomies, and heaven only knew what Mr Thomley-Jones might find or what he would say if he found anything. . . She sighed, got into the gown a nurse was offering on the end of the Cheatles and stood while it was tied.

Mr Reeves, the Registrar, was scrubbing too. 'Going on holiday today?' he wanted to know. 'Tom said something about a fishing trip. . .'

Amelia was putting on her rubber gloves. 'Yes—he's only got a week, though. I've got three—still, a week's better than nothing. I'm looking forward to it.'

'So's he, I imagine.' He glanced at her

carefully drawing the cuffs of her gloves over the sleeves of her gown. A nice girl and very pretty. Plenty of money too   and a good theatre Sister; he'd never seen her hesitate or falter or lose her temper for that matter, although he fancied that she could do that on occasion. A little cool for his taste, though — no, cool wasn't quite the word; reserved was better. He wondered if she was like that with Tom Crouch; it seemed to him that the pair of them hardly struck sparks. . .

Mr Thomley-Jones' voice, thick with annoyance, cut through his thoughts. 'Here I am, working my fingers to the bone and nothing ready,' he said as he entered the scrubbing up room.

It was Amelia who spoke, on her way out to the theatre, 'Everything is quite ready, sir,' she said briskly, and, 'Good morning, sir.'

'Oh, pooh, you've always got an answer, haven't you? Where's that fool of a young Phillips?'

'Your house surgeon is in theatre, sir.'

'Wretched girl, why are you smiling?'

'I think it's relief, sir, because we're quite ready for you.'

He laughed then and started to scrub. 'Go away, Amelia—in another minute I shall be in a good temper, and that'll never do!'

But miraculously, he stayed positively sunny for the entire morning. Even the discovery that the first laparotomy exposed a diverticulitis of magnitude and the second revealed a nasty patch of gangrene which he instantly removed made no difference. The list ran late, of course, and Amelia got no dinner in consequence, but that hardly mattered; there was only the afternoon's list to get through and Sybil would be relieving her at five o'clock. Amelia gobbled toast and drank mugs of tea in her office and went to scrub up.

The afternoon list wasn't a long one. They were finished by five o'clock and by half past that hour she had bidden Sybil goodbye, gone to the home for a cup of tea and then up to her room. She was driving herself down that evening, for Tom was still on duty and would meet them at Heathrow in the morning. She had snatched a brief moment with him on the way to the home and they had been able to make last-minute arrangements. She dressed now happily enough. A week in Tom's company would be lovely and give them a chance to talk; sometimes she wondered uneasily if, even when they were together, they talked about the right things. When they had first become engaged, they had discussed the future pretty thoroughly, but now it was as though having said it all once, there was no need to mention it again. Once or twice she had tried to persuade Tom to get married at once, but although he had been patient and understanding, he had been quite adamant—

perhaps being together would help to change his mind.

She got into the sage green tweed Jaeger suit she had bought only a week ago, quite forgetting that she wasn't going to wear anything new for a while. It had a pleated skirt and was warm enough to travel in with the matching cashmere sweater underneath. She had already filled her handbag with all the things she would require on the journey. She sprayed herself with Miss Dior, pushed her feet into beautifully made brown leather brogues, found her gloves and went down to the corner of the courtyard where the staff kept their cars. It was dark by now and in the headlights the hospital looked grim and very gloomy. Amelia swung the Mini out of the front gates and edged it carefully into the evening traffic.

Bonny had a late supper waiting for her. She ate it from a tray on a small sofa table in the drawing room while her father sat opposite her outlining his plans for the next three weeks. He had got them rooms at the hotel, he told her, arranged for the hire of a boat and had worked out some sort of an itinerary. 'We might as well see something of the country while we're there,' he told her. 'Not too far,' he added hastily, 'the best fishing is in that part, I'm told.'

It all sounded delightful. Presently Amelia went to bed, to sleep soundly until she was roused in the morning by Fred, her father's labrador, who expected to be taken for a quick walk before breakfast.

They left early with Badger sitting beside Mr Crosbie in front; he would drive the Bentley back home again and come to fetch them on their return. Amelia, sitting in the back, daydreamed gently. It would be perfect weather, of course, even if chilly, and Tom and she would hire a car and explore. She was certain that her father wouldn't mind at all if he were left to fish on his own; he'd been doing it for years and she suspected that although he tolerated her company he wasn't quite happy about Tom. They liked each other well enough. . . She frowned a little and switched her thoughts to the pleasanter one of the future—the wedding, the house they would find together and furnish and should she take Cordon Bleu cooking lessons or would Bonny be able to teach her how to cook? She wondered how much money she would need to housekeep; it was deplorable, but she really didn't know.

Tom reached Heathrow five minutes after they arrived there themselves; he parked his car, picked up his case and joined them quietly, shaking hands with her father and smiling at her as he held hers briefly. After her daydreaming it seemed rather a let-down.

She didn't like flying, but it saved time, and as the plane was only half full, she didn't get the feeling that she was travelling in a rather crowded bus. The weather was good too; England disappeared and with nothing but the sea below to look at she turned to Tom beside her. He was asleep and she smiled gently; probably he'd missed most of the night's rest and it must have been an almighty rush to get to the airport. She sat back quietly until the stewardess came round with the lunch trays and wakened Tom.

And almost before they had finished their coffee they were coming down over the countless islands round Bergen. The weather wasn't so good now, grey and great blankets of cloud which enveloped them until they touched down, when Amelia wasn't surprised to find that it was raining.

But who cared? she asked Tom as they followed her father into the arrival hall. They were on holiday.

CHAPTER TWO

THEY were to spend the night at the Norge hotel and leave the following morning by an air taxi Mr Crosbie had booked previously. Amelia would have preferred to have travelled to Stokmarknes by boat or road, but her father had come to fish and that as soon as possible. However, they had the rest of the day in which to explore Bergen and once settled into their rooms, she declared her intention of seeing as much of the town as she could.

'It's raining,' objected her father.

'I've got my anorak,' she pointed out reasonably. 'Besides, you know quite well that you'll not mind in the least if it rains every day once you get a rod in your hands.' She smiled at him and made for the door with Tom close behind her. 'We'll be back in plenty of time for dinner.'

They set off, walking the few yards down Ole Bulls Plass into the main shopping street, Torgalm, a wide thoroughfare with broad pavements and trees bordering them, only now there were few leaves and those that were left were limp with the rain. But the shops were splendid, their lights welcome in the early gloom of the afternoon. Amelia strolled along, her arm tucked into Tom's, pausing to look at everything until presently she suggested that they found somewhere for tea. 'Just a cup,' she begged. 'It's only four o'clock and it might be fun. I'm going to ask in this shop.'

There was a tea-room close by, the sales-lady told her in excellent English, and they found it without difficulty, a little way away from the shops, opposite a small beautifully kept park close to the hotel. Inside it lived up to its name with little tables occupied by smart housewives and uniformed waitresses, and to Amelia's satisfaction the tea was delicious and brought in a tea-pot, nicely set out with cups and saucers, and with it they ate enormous creamy cakes which Tom warned her would spoil her appetite for dinner later on.

'Oh, pooh,' she told him robustly, 'I'm a big girl and I get hungry.'

They wandered back presently and spent the rest of the evening in the hotel, eating deliciously in a beautifully appointed res-taurant. Amelia went to bed very contented, sure that the holiday was going to be one of the best she had ever spent.

They flew to Ardenes by air taxi the next morning and then went by hired car down to Stokmarknes. Amelia, who had heard of the Lofoten Islands but never been near them before, was struck dumb by the awe-inspiring scenery. The mountains loomed majestically almost to the edge of the fjords already deeply snow-capped, only here and there small green patches, each with its tiny community, clung to their skirts. Sitting behind the Norwegian driver as he followed the one road across the islands, she began to wonder what Stokmarknes would be like.

It was a delightful surprise. True, there was the inevitable fish oil refinery down by the small quay, but the little town itself, strung out along the fjord for perhaps a mile, was charming; its wooden houses, brightly painted and surrounded by birch trees, already orange and red-leafed, bordered each side of the road which ran on through the cluster of houses and small shops, towards Melbu and the Ferry. The hotel, close to the quay, was a square wooden building and Amelia's heart sank a little when she got out of the car before its door; it looked lonely and uninviting from where she stood. But inside she saw how wrong she had been; it was cosily warm for a start, bright with cheerful lights and comfortable modern furniture, and moreover they were welcomed by a smiling manager whose English was almost as good as theirs. There were, he told them cheerfully, very few visitors, but it was hardly the time of year, although to a keen fisherman that would make no difference, and, he went on, glancing at Amelia, there were some delightful walks in the neighbourhood and a daily bus service. Sortland or Svolvaer were no distance away by road. Meanwhile he would show them to their rooms and doubtless they would enjoy a cup of tea or coffee.

It was going to be great fun after all, she decided, looking with approval round her bedroom. It faced the fjord, so that she could see the constant coming and going on the water, and its furniture, though simple, was very much to her taste. She made short work of tidying herself and went downstairs to find the two men were already in the lounge, deep in discussion with the manager about the hiring of a boat. She heard her father's satisfied grunt when he was told that the vessel was ready and waiting for him.

'First thing tomorrow morning,' he promised Amelia, 'we'll take her out and see what we can get.' He glanced at Tom. 'You'll come, of course, Tom?'

'I'll be delighted, though I'm not much good with boats, I'm afraid.'

'Oh, never mind that,' said Crosbie in high good humour. 'Amelia is a first class crew, she'll tell you what to do. I understand the weather's likely to be good for a few days at least—they've had one or two snow showers further north, but they haven't reached these parts, although it'll probably rain.'

Amelia caught Tom's eye and smiled and was a little disconcerted to see that although he smiled back, he didn't look quite happy.

'Tom and I are going to do a bit of exploring once you've got your eye in, Father,' she said quickly. 'You're bound to find several enthusiasts before long, and I daresay they'll crew for you – besides, when Tom goes back I'll come out with you every day.'

She turned away to pour out the tea and her father answered her vaguely, his mind already busy with the question of how to get the most out of his stay.

Amelia and Tom went for a walk before dinner. It was already dusk, but the little place was well lighted, and they went from one end of the town to the other, admiring the houses, dotted haphazardly on either side of the road, creeping as far as they could go to the very edge of the fjord on one side, and on the other, tucking themselves against the base of the massive mountains.

'I could live here,' declared Amelia. 'It's peaceful and cosy and. . .'

'A bit isolated,' finished Tom. 'Nowhere to go in the evenings, is there?'

'Ah, I'd sit at home and embroider those lovely tapestries we saw in Bergen, and knit.'

He laughed at her. 'What? No dinners out, no cinemas, no theatre—you'd get bored.'

'No.' She suddenly felt a little irritated with him. 'I don't believe the people who live here are bored, I think they're content and satisfied with their lives——how could you be anything else with all this glorious scenery around?' She added a shade defiantly, 'I like it.'

Tom took her arm and turned her round to go back to the hotel. 'Well, so do I,' he said placatingly. 'I'm looking forward to tomorrow.'

It was a splendid morning; blue sky and a cold sun with almost no wind. They breakfasted together and then went down to the boat, not as early as Mr Crosbie would have liked, but Amelia had wanted to sample the variety of breads and rolls arranged on the long table in the restaurant, and try the contents of the great number of dishes laid upon it. She had never had herrings in an onion sauce for breakfast, nor beetroot and cucumber. The cold meats and cheese seemed more like home as well as the great bowl of marmalade, flanked by cranberry jam. She tried as many of them as possible and declared that she would get up earlier in future so that she might have a go at the rest.

But there was little fear of them going hungry, judging by the size of the picnic box they had been given to take with them. Amelia arranging things just so in the small cabin, found it all very satisfactory and great fun. It was going to be choppy later on, they had been warned, but she didn't mind that; she was wearing slacks stuffed into wellingtons, a bright yellow anorak and a wool cap pulled well down over her ears and thick gloves.

They cast off and her father started the outboard motor before leaving it to Tom's care while he went off to check his rods and bait. Today, he had assured them, was merely a trial run; they would go north through the fjord towards Sortland and see if there were any fish.

There were a great many. Presently Tom left Amelia to steer in the little cockpit while he joined her father, and presently she stopped the motor and they anchored while the two men reeled in trout, herring, flounders and a couple of salmon. It was past midday by then and she gave them their lunch, made soup and coffee on the stove and joined them on deck to listen patiently to their enthusiastic discussions as to which rod and what bait were the best to use. It was nice to see her father so happy and Tom too. She looked around her and could find no fault in her morning.

It began to rain a little by mid-afternoon and they turned for home, slowed by a sharp wind. Mr Crosbie was at the wheel now, thoroughly enjoying himself, not minding the change in the weather, although Tom looked a little uneasy. It was getting dark already and it was no use trying to use the binoculars

Amelia had brought with her. They stood side by side watching the lights of Stokmarknes getting nearer. The little quay, when they reached it, was almost deserted. The coastal steamer had come and gone and the little school was empty of children; only the shops were still open as they walked the short distance to the hotel. Amelia paused to buy a yesterday's *Telegraph* at the little kiosk close to the quay; the woman who served her was friendly and spoke a little English and she would have liked to have stayed a few minutes and talked, but the men were impatient now and hurried her along the road and in through the hotel door.

They ate their dinner with splendid appetites and Amelia went early to bed. The hotel manager had told them that a short walk in the morning would take them behind the little town and up the lower slopes of the mountains where the view of the fjord was something worth seeing, and Amelia persuaded her father to delay his fishing trip for an hour so that she and Tom might go. Her father hadn't minded; he had the rest of the short day to look forward to and there was a man who worked down on the quay who would tell him just where he could go for salmon.

Amelia, getting sleepily ready for bed, yawned widely and decided that she was enjoying herself hugely.

The morning walk was all that she had hoped for. They had turned off the road and taken a rocky lane leading up to the houses clinging so precariously to the lower slopes of the mountains. There were no roads here, only paths leading from one house to the next, and they had been built in haphazard charm between the birch trees. They left them behind presently, climbing over the rough ground, and then stopped to admire the view. It was cold, too, with a sky filled with clouds which every now and then allowed the sun to shine through. Amelia had brought the binoculars with her and used them now, picking out isolated houses along the shore. 'It's cold enough for snow,' she declared.

'A bit early for that,' observed Tom, 'though I must say it's rather wintry.' He smiled at her. 'Rather different from St Ansell's.'

She said impulsively: 'Tom, let's come here on our honeymoon,' and was chilled by his careless:

'Isn't it a bit too early to make plans?'

She said tonelessly: 'Yes, of course, I was only joking. We'd better get back or Father will get impatient.'

Walking back briskly, she kept the conversation cheerful and impersonal. Tom didn't want to talk about their future together, that was obvious. Perhaps she was too impatient, she must remember that; perhaps, she thought uneasily, she wanted her own way too much.

Her father was sitting on the rough stone wall bordering the road, his back to them, looking out to the fjord and talking to someone—a man who when he saw them, got to his feet, unfolding his great height slowly. He was broad-shouldered and heavily built as well as tall, with a handsome face whose eyes were heavy-lidded above an imposing nose. His hair was dark, as far as she could see, and his eyes as he frankly appraised Amelia were very blue.

She didn't like his stare. She lifted her chin and looked down her straight little nose, at the same time taking in the fact that he was wearing corduroy slacks stuffed into boots and a fisherman's waterproof jacket. Another fisherman, she thought, and how like Father to find him! He's probably the only one for miles around and they had to meet—and I don't like him, she told herself.

Her parent was in high good humour. 'Hullo, my dear,' he beamed at her. 'You see I've found another enthusiast. This is Doctor van der Tolck from Holland, like us, on holiday. My daughter Amelia and her fiancé, Doctor Tom Crouch.' He stood back smiling while they shook hands and murmured politely, and Amelia, meeting the Dutchman's sleepy gaze, had a sudden strange feeling, as though everything had changed; that nothing would ever be the same again; that there was no one else there, only herself and this giant of a man, still staring at her. She put out a hand and caught Tom's sleeve in a fierce grip which made him glance at her in surprise. Tom was there, right beside her, and she was going to marry him. . .

The man smiled faintly, just as though he read her thoughts and mocked them, and made some remark to Tom. She told herself, seconds later, that she had imagined the whole puzzling thing.

'Doctor van der Tolck has a boat here too,' observed Mr Crosbie with satisfaction. 'He's staying at the hotel, got here last night on the coastal express. We might go out together— he tells me that the Raftsund is a good area for cod.'

'What are we going to do with the catch?' asked Amelia.

'Oh, let the hotel people have it,' declared her parent carelessly. 'Well, how about moving off?'

She took a quick peep at the Dutchman, who was standing quietly, saying nothing, apparently waiting for the rest of them.

'We'll go and pick up the food,' she offered, and gave Tom's sleeve a tug. 'Tom?'

'Do that, my dear, and ask them to let you have Doctor van der Tolck's sandwiches at the same time.'

'I have to go back to the hotel,' he had a slow deep voice, 'I'll pick my food up then.'

He smiled at Mr Crosbie. 'Shall I come down to the quay with you—you were going to show me that rod of yours.'

Amelia turned away with Tom beside her. On the way to the hotel she said with a touch of pettishness: 'Why on earth does Father have to dig up these chance acquaintances—I expect he'll stick like a leech now!'

'You don't like him?'

'No, I do not,' she said a little too sharply, 'butting in like that.'

'Probably your father suggested that we should join forces—rather difficult to refuse in the circumstances.'

'Rubbish, Tom—he could have made some excuse.'

He gave her a long considered look. 'You do dislike him, don't you?'

She bounced through the hotel door. 'Yes,' she snapped. 'I shall keep out of his way.'

A decision which Doctor van der Tolck had apparently made too, for he had little or nothing to say to her when she and Tom rejoined him and her father presently—polite enough, but she mistrusted the wicked gleam in his eyes and the faint smile when he spoke to her, which he did only when politeness made it imperative.

He left them presently, agreeing easily with Mr Crosbie that he would join them in his own boat within ten minutes. He was as good as his word, manoeuvring it alongside their own vessel while he exchanged opinions with Mr Crosbie as to the best area in which to fish. They settled the important question at last, working their way down towards the Raftsund and presently they anchored, not too far apart, and settled down to the serious business in hand. The clouds had strengthened and the sun no longer shone even fitfully, the mountains around them were grey and cold and Amelia secretly found them a little frightening. She went into the cabin and made coffee and sat there in comparative warmth, drinking it after handing out mugs to her father and Tom. The doctor, she saw out of the corner of her eye, had a thermos flask and even at a distance was a picture of contentment.

The weather worsened as the day went on and by three o'clock it was disagreeably cold and windy. Mr Crosbie reluctantly conceded the wisdom of returning to dry land before the rain, falling gently so far, became torrential. But he had had a good day; he and Tom sorted their catch while Amelia took the wheel. She was good at it. She passed their new acquaintance within a few feet, sending the boat tearing through the dark water before he had even got his engine going. It was galling, half way there, to be overtaken. He was making fast as she approached the quay and without speaking to her, performed the same service for her, and when she thanked him, rather haughtily, he grunted.

She left the three men there, telling each other fishy tales while they gloated over their catches, and went up to the hotel, where she ordered tea in her room and had a bath, far too hot.

It was difficult to avoid Doctor van der Tolck. The hotel wasn't large and except for a couple of commercial travellers and a rather subdued family—on their way, the manager confided, to a funeral on the outskirts of the town—they were the only guests. True, by the time she had joined her father and Tom in the bar, a trickle of young men with their girls came in, but they kept to themselves although they were friendly enough. Amelia, sipping her sherry, made idle conversation and kept an eye on the door. Doctor van der Tolck was just the kind of man to join them for the evening unasked.

She was mistaken. He sauntered in presently, nodded pleasantly and joined the two Norwegians at the bar and either he spoke their language or they spoke Dutch, because they entered into a lengthy conversation and Amelia, her ears stretched, was sure that it wasn't English they were speaking. It was annoying when he looked up suddenly and caught her looking at them, and still more annoying that he didn't smile.

He dined at a table alone too, and she was

a little surprised that her father hadn't asked him to join them. She didn't say anything, but when her father said casually: 'I didn't ask van der Tolck to join us—I hear from Tom that you don't like him,' she went pink and shot Tom a peevish look which in the circumstances was quite unjustified.

But he was there in the morning. She had gone out before breakfast to inspect the high slender bridge which joined Stokmarknes with the neighbouring island of Langoya. It was a bit too far to walk to, she saw with regret, but perhaps she and Tom would get a chance to reach it later in the day. She had supposed that it was much nearer, but appearances were deceptive, and even though she hurried to where the houses began to peter out against the base of the mountains, the bridge seemed as far away as ever. She turned round with regret and started back to the hotel, picking her way carefully along the uneven road. She hadn't gone a quarter of the distance when a Saab swept past her and then stopped. Doctor van der Tolck was driving and Amelia said good morning in a cool voice as she drew abreast of him. He held the door open. 'Like a lift?' he enquired in a voice which suggested that he couldn't care less either way. 'I'm going back for breakfast.'

'Thank you.' She got in without argument. She had vowed to avoid him, but he was exactly the kind of man to demand to know why she refused if she did. He leaned across to slam the door shut and drove on without saying a word. What a good thing, she thought sourly, that the drive was a short one, for she couldn't think of anything to say even if he had been disposed to make conversation. She peeped at him from under her lashes. He looked inscrutable—a silly, novelish word but it did describe the expression of his profile. A rather splendid profile too; a pity she didn't like him. If he had been friendly it would have been nice to have talked. . . She had Tom, she reminded herself happily, and smiled quite nicely at her companion as they stopped at the hotel and he opened the door for her.

'Thanks for the lift,' she said cheerfully. 'I daresay we shall be seeing each other very shortly.'

He agreed politely, but his smile disconcerted her; it was for all the world as though he had a secret joke which amused him very much and that after she had held out the olive branch— well not exactly held it out, but. . . She let the thought slide away; it was a great pity that she couldn't opt out of the day's fishing trip.

She did indeed suggest to Tom that they should take the bus to Sortland and have a look round, and they were arguing gently about it when Doctor van der Tolck came over to their table to speak to her father and he, despite a heavy frown from his daughter, at once suggested that the two of them should join forces for the day. 'For Amelia is dead set on going to Sortland and of course Tom will go with her. There's a bus. . .'

'A splendid idea,' agreed the doctor, so promptly that she suspected that he would be glad to see the back of her. He turned to Tom. 'I've a Saab outside --rented it for my stay— why not borrow it? The road runs alongside the fjord and is pretty good going. There's a bridge at Sortland and you can cross over to Hinney Island and visit Harstad; it's quite a sizeable place and a military headquarters.' He added, glancing at Amelia, 'A street of shops, too.'

The faintly mocking glance he gave her from under his lids instantly made her change her mind. 'Perhaps another day,' she said coolly, to be overruled by Tom's:

'That's jolly decent of you, if the weather changes we might not get another chance, and I'll be going back in three days' time.'

Amelia poured herself some more coffee which she didn't want, but it was something to do while she argued. 'Yes, but what about you, Father?'

Her parent was of no help at all. 'Oh, we'll manage very well, my dear—you and Tom go off and enjoy yourselves together.'

'Yes, but you can't manage the boat alone,' she persisted.

'Who said I was going to? We'll use mine and share a picnic lunch. If the weather holds we shan't come back before four o'clock, so don't hurry on our account.'

The day had not been a qualified success. Amelia, soaking herself in a hot bath that evening, mulled it over at leisure and tried to decide where it had gone wrong. They had started off well enough—indeed, the drive to Sortland had been pleasant. The road, just as the doctor had told them, had followed the fjord the whole way and Sortland, when they reached it, was charming. They had coffee there, walked around the village, and then decided to go on to Harstad, so they drove over the bridge to the neighbouring island, Hinney, and took the only road, at first following the fjord and then going inland and taking a ferry once again. It proved to be a longer journey than they had expected and when they got to Harstad it was raining. They lunched at the Viking Nordic and then walked along the main street, looking at the shops, and Amelia, determined to take back some token of their trip, spent far too long in a rather splendid bookshop where she bought a couple of paperbacks, some writing paper and a pen she didn't really need. Tom bought nothing at all, waiting patiently while she pottered round the shelves, and it was almost three o'clock when he suggested mildly that they should think about getting back to Stokmarknes.

And none too soon. The rain had settled down to a steady drizzle and the sky was an unrelieved grey, merging with the mountains, their snowy tops completely hidden by cloud. 'We'll have tea in Sortland,' suggested Tom as they started back, but by the time they had reached it, it was dark, Tom was quietly apprehensive and Amelia becoming short-tempered. The day had been a waste. They hadn't talked about themselves at all; her secret hopes that with time on their hands they could have got their future settled were coming to nothing. Tom was in no mood to talk about weddings -- indeed, he had never been less romantic, advising her somewhat tersely to keep a sharp eye on the road, which, now that it was dark, wasn't nearly as easy as it had been that morning.

They arrived back at the hotel at six o'clock, relieved to be there but unable to be lighthearted about it and meeting the doctor in the foyer didn't help matters. He was sitting comfortably reading a Dutch newspaper, a drink at his elbow, but he got up as they went in, enquired kindly if they had enjoyed their day, expressed regret at the weather and invited them to have a drink. Tom, after a glance at Amelia, accepted, but she refused, declaring she wanted a cup of tea before she did anything else.

The doctor obligingly pressed the bell for her. 'No tea?' he asked with what she decided was quite false sympathy. 'There's a good hotel in Sortland.'

'We left Harstad rather late,' she explained stiffly, and when a waitress came asked for tea to be brought to her room, to drink it under the doctor's amused eye was more than she could manage.

But tea and the bath soothed her, so that by the time she got downstairs she was feeling quite cheerful again. Tom was already there, so she went across the bar to him and tucked her hand into his arm. 'Sorry if I was a bit snappy,' she said softly. 'It was disappointing, wasn't it—all that rain.'

He agreed placidly and ordered her a drink, moving a little way away so that she had to take her hand away, and she frowned a little. Tom hated any form of affectionate display in public and just for the moment she had forgotten that. Amelia perched herself on a stool at the bar and began a rather banal conversation with the barman and Tom and they were presently joined by her father and Doctor van der Tolck, both with the air of men who had enjoyed every minute of their day and were now prepared to enjoy their evening just as much. And strangely enough, the evening was so pleasant that she had gone

reluctantly to bed, much later than usual.
Doctor van der Tolck had joined them for
dinner and proved himself to be an amusing
companion without attempting to hog the
conversation—indeed, his aptitude for listening with interest to whatever was being said
contributed to the success of the evening and
even Amelia, wary of his friendly manner,
found herself telling him about St Ansell's.
She only just stopped herself in time from
telling him that she intended continuing to
work there after she and Tom were married.
She had told him too much already. . . .

She stopped almost in mid-sentence
and asked: 'Are you married, Doctor van
der Tolck?'

He had dropped his lids so that she
couldn't see his eyes. He said evenly: 'No,
I am not. Shall you be going fishing
tomorrow?'

It was a palpable snub and she flushed a
little, admitting to herself that she had
deserved it. All the same, thinking about it
afterwards, she came to the conclusion that
while he had extracted quite a lot of information about her, he had said precious little
about himself. Not that she was in the least
interested.

She avoided him as much as possible for
the next two days, although he shared their
table now, to her father's pleasure and to
her own unease, but she had Tom to talk to,

although not for much longer now, since he would be leaving the next day, and she wondered once or twice if it would be a good idea if she went back with him. She even suggested it, to be met with a very natural surprise on Tom's part. 'What on earth for?' he wanted to know. 'Your father would be left on his own and you know he wanted you to go with him in the first place.'

'Yes, well—there's Doctor van der Tolck to keep him company.'

Tom shook his head. 'He told me that he was going further north after salmon.'

She told herself that she was delighted at the news. 'Oh, well, then I'll stay.'

'You won't be bored?'

She shook her head. 'We'll be out for most of the day and I'm going to buy some of that lovely embroidery to do—I should have got some in Harstad. I'll persuade Father to take the ferry and we'll spend a day there—a change from fishing will do him good.' She added, trying not to sound too eager: 'Will you miss me, Tom?'

'I'll be up to my eyes in work,' he told her, which wasn't a very satisfactory answer. 'There's that team of Australian physicians coming over at the end of the week, it'll be interesting to work with them. I heard that there's a strong chance that they'll offer jobs to any of us who are interested.' He glanced at her, 'How do you like the idea of Australia, Amelia?'

She shook her head. 'Me? Not at all—so far away.' She turned to look at him. 'Tom, you're not serious, are you?'

'Why not? There are marvellous opportunities out there. We'll discuss it when you get back.'

They were in the lounge waiting for her father and Doctor van der Tolck.

'Why not now?' she asked.

'Oh, plenty of time for that,' Tom said easily.

They almost never quarrelled, but now Amelia felt herself on the verge of it.

'But there's not, Tom—you're thirty and I'm twenty-seven and we haven't even made any plans. . .'

'Oh, come on, old girl—you know I can't make plans until I've got a really good job. Another year or two—that's not long, especially as we're both working—no time to brood.'

'I'll be nudging thirty,' said Amelia in a voice which held faint despair. She would have said more, only her father came in then, rubbing his hands and declaring that it was getting decidedly chilly and how about coffee before they started out. 'We're going down beyond the bridge,' he told them enthusiastically, 'they say there's any amount of cod there.'

They were joined a moment later by the doctor, who drank his coffee with them but hadn't much to say for himself, and presently they all trooped out and went down to the boats. It was getting colder, thought Amelia, glad of her quilted jacket and hood, and she prayed for clear skies. Bad weather wouldn't keep her father indoors, and although he was cheerfully impervious to wind and rain, the idea of sitting in a smallish boat for hours on end in anything less than moderately fine weather daunted her.

But they were lucky for the moment. The sun came out and the mountains, with the gold and red of the birch trees wreathed around their lower slopes, didn't look so forbidding, and the sun turned their snowy tops to a glistening fairyland, at least from a distance. The water was calm, dark and cold, but the three men didn't notice that. They fished with enthusiasm, accepting hot drinks and food when Amelia proffered them, although she had the strong suspicion that they had quite forgotten that she was there. But not quite, apparently; it was the early afternoon when Doctor van der Tolck put his head round the cabin door where she was washing cups in the minute sink to ask her if she was all right. 'We'll have to get back fairly soon,' he told her, 'the light's going and it's getting cold.'

To which moderate remark she gave polite

answer. As far as she was concerned it had got cold hours ago.

As it was Tom's last evening, dinner was something of an event. They are some of the cod they had caught with a rich creamy soup to precede it and reindeer steaks to follow, and rounded off the meal with chocolate mousse and coffee. And the doctor insisted on a bottle of wine, which, on top of the sherry she had had before dinner, warmed her very nicely.

They went to sit round the square stove afterwards, but not for long, for the doctor had offered to drive Tom to the airport at Ardenes in the morning and they would have to make an early start.

Amelia went to bed presently with the promise that she would be down in the morning to say goodbye to Tom. She was going to miss him, but two weeks would soon pass. She bade him a rather matter-of-fact goodnight because Doctor van der Tolck was watching them and hoped that he would have the good sense to look the other way when they said goodbye.

And strangely enough, he did. They breakfasted early and she joined them for a cup of coffee. Almost at once he got to his feet with some remark about the car and went away, leaving her and Tom looking at each other.

'Well, it's been a lovely week,' said Amelia.

'I enjoyed it enormously—I had no idea that fishing could be so absorbing.' Tom caught her eye and added hastily, 'It was splendid having you here too.'

'I'll be back in two weeks—I wish I were coming with you, or that you could have stayed for the rest of the time.'

'Well, we knew that before we started, didn't we?' Tom got to his feet and went to put on his jacket lying ready. 'I'd better be off, mustn't miss the plane.' He looked around him and then kissed her; there was no one there and there was no need to be so brisk about it, Amelia thought unhappily. She said: 'Oh, Tom. . .' and then at the look of faint unease on his nice face: 'All right, I'm not going to cry or anything like that.' She managed a bright smile and saw his relief. She kept it there while he went through the door.

CHAPTER THREE

HER father took one look at her rather set face, declared that they might just as well get their lunch basket and be on their way, and bustled off to get his fishing gear, which gave Amelia time to get her pretty face back into its usual serene lines, and when he appeared presently she was able to give enthusiastic answers to his remarks about the day's sport. 'A pity van der Tolck won't be back—still, we should get a good day's fishing before the light changes. We won't be back too late—the manager tells me that there's a dance this evening, and I daresay you'll like to go.'

She tried to sound cheerful. 'But, Father, you hate dancing, and Tom's not here.'

'Well, I daresay van der Tolck won't mind waltzing you round a couple of times.'

'Waltzing is old-fashioned,' said Amelia tartly. 'Besides, I shall probably go to bed early.'

A remark which she repeated to the doctor when they returned to the hotel. After an inevitable résumé of the day's activities, he had asked her pleasantly enough if she cared to go to the dance after dinner and she had been a little vexed at his placid acceptance of her refusal. Indeed, she had the strong impression that having done his duty in asking her, he was relieved at her answer. She waited for ten minutes, half listening to their earnest talk as they bent over a map, and when they paused, said sweetly: 'I think I'll change my mind. It might be fun to dance for half an hour or so.'

His 'Splendid', sounded to her critical ears half-hearted.

She wore the burgundy jersey dress and thanked heaven that she had remembered to pack a pair of high-heeled shoes. The dress was plain but beautifully cut and she took pains with her face and hair and found herself looking forward to the evening after all. Probably the doctor danced badly; he must be all of fifteen stone and she hadn't seen him hurry even once, probably he was lazy. She had to admit to herself that that wasn't true. Lazy men didn't get up at first light and spend the day in a small boat, and presumably if he had a practice, he would need the energy to run it. She would ask him during the evening just what he did do. There were doctors and doctors.

She had no chance to find out anything. He countered her carefully put questions with a faintly amused ease which was distinctly annoying and surprised her very much by being easily the best dancer in the room, and most of them were good. Amelia danced well herself and presently, despite her feelings, she began to enjoy herself. The place was full. Obviously dancing was a favourite pastime in Stokmarknes; moreover there was a band, not a tape recorder, and they swung easily from waltzes and foxtrots to jive, and finally to the local dances which they were persuaded to join in.

'Oh, what fun!' Amelia's face was flushed and her eyes bright and her neat head was ruffled. Her companion gave her a long look. 'Yes—such a pity that Tom isn't here to share it with you.'

His voice told her nothing, but her flush deepened. 'Yes,' she added defiantly. 'We go dancing quite a bit—it's a pity he missed those last dances.' And her companion didn't answer: 'Thank you for a pleasant evening. I'm rather tired, I'll got to bed, I think.'

'So soon?' He glanced at the clock and she saw with a shock that they had been dancing for more than two hours. She said lightly: 'How time passes when one is. . .' She had been going to say enjoying oneself, but how could she have when she didn't like him?

'Dancing?' he supplied blandly.

She nodded and wished him goodnight. Truth to tell, she could have danced for the rest of the night, but not, she told herself firmly, with him. As she got ready for bed she went over her evening. She had learned exactly nothing about the doctor, the vague answers he had given her had left her as much in the dark as she ever had been. She would have to ask her father.

But when she went down to breakfast the next morning it was to find her parent far too busy with his own affairs to take any interest in her questions. 'It's simply splendid,' he observed after wishing her a hasty good morning. 'Van der Tolck tells me he's rented a boat for fishing the Alta river. He's moving up there in two days' time and suggested that we might like to go with him. Best fishing in the world, my dear, I can hardly believe my luck.'

Amelia thought of a great deal to say to this but prudently thought better of it. 'Where is the Alta river?' she asked.

'A good bit further north, but of course we'd go in his car. There's a good road, you know, the E6. It'll take a day or two to get there, of course, but we've still got two weeks and the idea is to fly back from Alta.' He beamed at her. 'Salmon, my dear, just about the best. . .'

'Did Doctor van der Tolck actually ask us to go with him?'

Her father looked surprised. 'Haven't I just said so, my dear? Ah, here he is now. Van der Tolck, Amelia seems to think that your invitation wasn't a genuine one.' He beamed at her over his glasses. 'Pour the doctor some coffee, Amelia.'

The doctor sat down opposite her, took his cup, wished them good morning and chose a roll. 'Perfectly genuine,' he observed placidly, 'and I hope that you will agree to come with us.' He glanced at her as he spoke, and Amelia was sure that he was laughing to himself again; he knew as well as she that there was nothing else that she could do. Stokmarknes was a dear little place, but just what would she do with herself if she elected to stay behind? Besides, if she did that it would amuse him still more to know that she was avoiding him. And she had no reason to do that, none at all, only of course she did dislike him, from the first moment she had set eyes upon him, and she had had that strange feeling. . .

'There is quite a good hotel at Alta,' said the doctor's voice quietly.

'Yes — well, of course I'll come. When exactly do you plan to go, Doctor?'

'My name is Gideon,' he told her. 'I had suggested two days' time, but I wondered if we might make it tomorrow? We can drive to Narvik and join the E6 highway and press on as far as possible; there are good inns along the Arctic Highway and with luck we should be able to stay at one of those. Provided that we leave in good time after a night's stop, we should get to Alta the following day. It isn't a town, you know, but a group of villages strung together, but there is, as I have said, a good hotel there. I'll telephone presently and see if they can give us rooms.'

He had it all organised, she realised, and he must have known about it days ago. Her father had remarked before they left England that the Alta river was one of the best fishing rivers in Norway and wildly expensive; too much even for his relatively deep pocket. She glanced at her parent, looking so pleased with life that she hadn't the heart to do more than fall in with a show of enthusiasm with their plans.

They left directly after breakfast on the following morning, the fishing gear loaded lovingly into the boot and overflowing into the back of the car where Amelia had elected to sit. The weather was bright and cold, but in the distance the snow-capped mountains were already hiding their tops in cloud. Probably they would meet bad weather as they went north, but the doctor shrugged this off carelessly, merely saying that they could always stop when they wanted to and wait for the weather to clear.

He drove well, Amelia decided, very fast when he could but taking hairpin bends and narrow stretches with calculated caution. The thought crept unwillingly into her head that Tom had been nothing like as good.

They stopped at Harstad for coffee, but they didn't waste time, pressing on to Narvik where they stopped for a rather late lunch at the Grand Hotel. Amelia would have liked to have stopped for a few hours and explored the town, but the two men were intent on getting as far as possible before dark. She was tucked up once more with a variety of fishing clobber and they set off, with, rather surprisingly, Tromso as their goal.

'I thought we were going to spend the night at an inn,' ventured Amelia.

'Well, it takes a day by bus to Tromso from Narvik, but of course the bus stops a good deal—the road's pretty good, but there are a number of ferries, which may hold us up.'

They made good time, although it was late and dark by the time they reached Tromso. It wasn't until they were sitting comfortably in the delightful lounge of the SAS Royal Hotel, having drinks before dinner, that Mr Crosbie, taking advantage of the doctor's absence for a moment, remarked, 'Gideon thought you might like a comfortable night and a good meal. Tromso is a little out of our way.'

Amelia felt surprise. 'How very kind of him—I shouldn't have thought. . . Well, never mind. I must say that this is pretty nice—I've got a very nice room too. Do we reach Alta tomorrow?'

Mr Crosbie laughed. 'I imagine so. It's been a long day today, hasn't it? We've been lucky with the weather, though, and Gideon knows how to drive.'

The doctor rejoined them then and presently they dined together, sitting over their coffee until Amelia went reluctantly to bed. She might not like Gideon, but she had to admit that he was an entertaining companion. She thought about him sleepily as she got ready for bed; it was only as she was on the verge of sleep that she remembered to give Tom a thought.

They left early the next morning before the shops had opened and Amelia stared with regret at the quiet streets. She would dearly have loved to have spent a day exploring them and browsing round the silversmiths and the tempting woollies on display. Perhaps on the way back. . .

'Do we have to fly back?' she asked presently.

It was Gideon who answered her. 'I should imagine so, but if you hanker for a day's shopping, we could fly down from Alta.'

She answered him tartly. 'It seems such a pity to come all this way and see nothing but fish!'

They stopped for coffee after they had crossed the second ferry, at Olderdalen, where the inn was surprisingly modern and comfortable, but they didn't waste time there but kept steadily on through a morning which, as it slid into afternoon, became increasingly grey. Indeed, by four o'clock with Burfjord and lunch behind them, it was almost dark. Gideon stopped the car presently and twisted round in his seat to look at Amelia.

'Do you feel like going on?' he asked. 'It isn't all that distance now and I imagine the hotel at Alta will be more comfortable than any wayside inn we may pass. There are no more villages or towns before Alta now.'

'Let's go on,' she declared. She was tired now, although the journey had been wonderful; she had never expected to see such breathtaking scenery, but a comfortable bed and a good dinner were tempting, even if they were still some way off.

Gideon started up the car without saying anything and she was left wondering what he would have said if she had declared that she wanted to stop at the very next inn, whatever it was like. He would have talked her out of it, she had no doubt of that.

Alta was a pleasant surprise when they arrived. It was dark by now, but Amelia was already used to the generous use of electricity even in the tiniest of communities, and Alta was no exception. And the hotel was surprisingly large and comfortable. She surveyed her room with pleasure and only stopping long enough to tidy herself went straight down for their late dinner. They ate magnificently—a creamy soup, followed by salmon, which after all was to be expected, and a large tiered cream cake to round them off. The two men drank an akvavit and beer, but Amelia, although she longed to try the fiery spirit, accepted a ladylike white wine with a good grace, and after coffee and half an hour's desultory talk, she said goodnight; it was clear to her that the men wanted to discuss their plans for the next day and she suspected that they were pleased enough to see her go.

It was a splendid morning with a blue sky and a cold wind which hinted at an icy winter not far off. They left the hotel directly after breakfast to go aboard the boat the doctor had hired. It was small and fast and held all the basic comforts, and Amelia, prowling round its tiny galley, nodded a satisfied head; she would be able to make coffee as often as it was needed, heat soup and wash up in comfort. They wasted no time. Almost before she had stowed their lunch away tidily they were off and she was being called on deck to take the tiller while the men got their rods ready.

The river was wide for the first few miles, but presently, when they had passed Gargia, the only other village for miles, it narrowed, and seemed more so by reason of the mountains nudging themselves to the very shores of it. But it wasn't lonely; there were other boats from time to time and great herds of reindeer being driven down to their winter pastures. Amelia stood for a long time watching them through binoculars and only her father's demands for coffee sent her to the cabin.

There was salmon enough; they returned back to the hotel in the gathering dusk, the men well pleased with themselves and Amelia agreeably surprised at the pleasure she had got out of the day's outing. It was later over dinner that the doctor suggested that they should go further the following day; there was an island, it seemed, where one could land and fish from its rocky shore. His, 'I daresay you might be bored, Amelia,' was uttered in such a tone of certainty that she immediately said that there was nothing she would rather do. . .

The island was easily found, although it was a good deal further than she had expected. They found a narrow shelf of ground, made fast to the stout pole someone had caused to be put there, and scrambled ashore. The island was only a few hundred yards across, bare rock for the most part, but here and there small hollows scooped out by wind and weather over the years, lined with lichen. The two men brought the food ashore and Amelia busied herself getting a meal while they wandered off, deep in discussion

as to the best place from where to do their
fishing. Indeed, they forgot all about lunch.
Amelia watched resignedly while they
climbed down to the water's edge and cast
their lines. It wasn't until they had each
caught a salmon that they remembered, rather
sheepishly, that she was waiting for them.

They had almost finished their picnic when
Amelia turned her face to the suddenly dark-
ening sky, scrambled to her splendid height,
and exclaimed: 'Rain!' in a gloomy voice and
then bent to gather up the remains of the
picnic tidily into the basket.

'Splendid,' declared Mr Crosbie; his voice
held real pleasure. 'Just what we need, eh,
Gideon?'

He got up too and started for the boat,
anxious to be off.

The doctor didn't answer but after a quick
look at the sky, swept the rest of the plates
and mugs pellmell into the basket. He did it
quickly and not very tidily and Amelia made
a disapproving sound.

'Yes, I know—not quite up to your stan-
dard, am I, dear girl? but better an untidy
basket than a sopping wet one.' His tone was
vaguely mocking and she curled her lip
at him.

'I like things done properly,' she told him
tartly, and then decided to say nothing more;
the rain was suddenly coming down in earnest now and she hurried to fasten her jacket

and pull up the hood. By the time she had done it he had flung everything into the basket and tossed it into the boat and come back to give her a hand over the slippery rocks.

But she disdained his help, took two steps and stumbled, to be hauled to her feet without him saying a word. It wasn't until they were on board that he paused to murmur: 'Pride comes before a fall, Amelia.'

She gave him a look to cut a lesser man to the bone, and: 'Don't say it,' he counselled kindly.

The rain settled down to a steady downpour from a sky which Amelia privately decided would deluge them with snow at any minute, but her companions hardly noticed; it was another two hours before they pronounced themselves satisfied with a splendid catch and ready to go home. She gave them mugs of scalding coffee, tidied the cabin and went to the tiller. But this time Gideon sent her back into the comparative warmth of the cabin, declaring that her father could deal with the gear while he sent the boat tearing down the river back to the hotel.

So there was nothing for Amelia to do but sit and think. Glancing outside into the murky afternoon, she wondered why she had ever come on this holiday with her father; it hadn't turned out at all as she had expected it to. True, she and Tom had had a very pleasant week together, although surely it should have been more than that? But she hadn't bargained for Gideon van der Tolck. He was, she told herself, the very last man she would have chosen to spend a holiday with—an hour, for that matter. He was always laughing silently at her, for a start, and making nasty remarks in that cool voice of his. Tom was a hundred times nicer. She concentrated fiercely on Tom and was disconcerted to find that his face had become curiously blurred in her memory; it was even more disconcerting to find that the doctor's handsome features wouldn't go away from her mind's eye. She got up and poked her head out into the wet in the hope that the rain would wash his face away, a process considerably helped by his harsh: 'Get inside, unless you want to be wet to your skin.'

If it would have been light enough for him to see her properly, she would have tossed her head at him, but it hardly seemed worth it. Back at last, she skipped on to the quay, disdaining his hand, and hurried into the hotel, where she spent the next hour or so lying in a hot bath and washing her hair. It was a pity that she hadn't brought more clothes with her, she thought, putting on the burgundy dress once more. All the same, she collected all eyes as she went into the bar, crowded with fishermen telling each other tall stories. Almost to a man they paused to look at her—all except Doctor van der Tolck, who although he got politely to his feet as she joined him and her father, gave her the briefest possible glance, like a man glancing at a clock and with just as much interest. Amelia's charming bosom swelled with annoyance.

But it was hard to remain aloof for more than a moment or so. The day had to be discussed from every angle, and the weights of the various fish gloated over, and it was inevitable that a number of those in the bar should gravitate to their corner. The talk was all of the day's sport, while Amelia, thankful to find a sprinkling of wives, exchanged pleasant gossip with them.

They broke up presently to go in to dinner and as they sat down Mr Crosbie said happily: 'There's an American here—had no luck at all.' He chuckled. 'He wanted to know if I'd show him the best places to go.'

Gideon interrupted smoothly: 'Why not do just that? Take my boat tomorrow.'

Mr Crosbie hesitated. 'But what about you? We're your guests.'

The doctor glanced at Amelia. 'It might be a good opportunity to fly down to Tromso. I'm sure Amelia wants to do some shopping and there are one or two enquiries I want to make.'

Amelia, her soup spoon half way to her mouth, stared at him, stopping herself just in time from asking what enquiries. 'We've only just got here,' she stated flatly.

He smiled. 'The weather could worsen any day now— we might not get another chance.'

'Yes, well—but I could shop on the way back.'

The two men exchanged glances. It was Mr Crosbie who spoke. 'Now, we've had a little chat about that—it seems a good idea if we fly back to Trondheim and then pick up the Coastal Steamer as far as Bergen— variety of scene,' he added airily. 'We shall see much more of the country.'

'But won't that take ages?'

'About three hours flying and a day at sea.' It was the doctor who answered her. 'You'll enjoy the coastline scenery.'

'It sounds very nice. And then we fly back from Bergen?' She wasn't looking at him but watching the waiter transfer a salmon steak on to her plate.

'If you have no objection,' observed the doctor in the smooth voice she was beginning to distrust, 'I have asked your father if you would both care to fly to Holland with me and spend a night at my home.'

Amelia put down her knife and fork very deliberately. 'But I have to get back to St Ansell's.'

'Naturally; there is no reason why you shouldn't. We can spend another four or five days here, and take another three days to reach my home and still have a couple of days in hand.'

She looked at her father who most provokingly beamed at her, just as though he considered she had been offered a rare treat. 'Rather a splendid idea, don't you think, my dear? Very kind of Gideon to ask us. I knew you'd like the idea.'

She was strongly of a mind to tell him that she didn't like the idea at all, although she wasn't sure why, but how could she without being rude and disappointing him?

'It sounds delightful,' she said woodenly, and caught the doctor's eye. He was laughing at her again even though he looked as bland as a judge.

'And what about tomorrow?' he persisted gently, 'unless of course you don't fancy flying?'

She ate some salmon and didn't answer him at once. 'If by that you mean am I frightened of flying—no, not particularly. I shall enjoy a day's shopping on my own.'

His blue eyes gleamed under their heavy lids. 'Splendid—the plane leaves about nine o'clock and there's one back in the afternoon, so we should be back here in time for dinner. Does that suit you?'

Amelia helped herself to some more shrimp sauce. 'Very nicely, thanks. You'll be all right, Father?'

'My dear girl, of course—I'll have this

American chap with me. Bring back some papers, will you? They might be a day earlier in Tromso.'

They began to talk about something else then and Amelia ate her apple cake wreathed in a pile of whipped cream and didn't take much part in the conversation. She felt peculiar—perhaps she shouldn't have had two sherries before dinner. She prudently refused a second glass of the excellent white burgundy they were drinking and decided that the feeling had nothing to do with drinking sherry; she wasn't sure what it was.

The feeling was still there when she went up to bed two hours later. She pooh-poohed the idea of excitement—what had she to be excited about? Certainly not the prospect of a journey with the tiresome doctor. She got into bed and wrote a long letter to Tom.

There was a letter from him in the morning, forwarded from Stokmarknes. She had no time to read it though, for they left after an early breakfast to drive to the airport so that she slipped it into her pocket to read later.

Which she did presently, sitting rather squashed by the doctor's bulk. The plane was full and everyone was talking to everyone else. Gideon, when he saw her take out the envelope, turned away to join in a conversation with two passengers across the aisle. Indeed, he left her in peace until the stewardess brought round the coffee and then enquired casually: 'Good news, I hope?'

Amelia hesitated. Tom's letter was hardly that; it was rather a bald account of his journey back and the variety of cases which had awaited him, and he finished with the statement that it had been a pleasant little interlude but he was glad to get back to work, although he was looking forward to seeing her soon.

'Well, just news,' she told him slowly, and put the letter away. Just for a moment she felt like telling him about Tom and herself, the future they had planned together, and over and above that, the small doubts and fears which she had been holding at bay for some time now, although she had never admitted it. She said, hardly knowing what she was saying: 'I love him very much.'

'Of course you do.' Gideon sounded cheerfully matter-of-fact. 'He's a lucky chap. Have one of these little biscuits—we'll be there very shortly.'

She was grateful to him for accepting her remark so placidly. She had been silly to have made it; perhaps he wasn't so bad after all.

She followed him out of the airport happily enough, got into the taxi he had hailed and found herself very shortly in the heart of Tromso.

'You'd rather be on your own?' asked the doctor kindly. 'We have six or seven hours, so there's no hurry. The shopping centre isn't large, but it's quite a good one. Shall we meet at the SAS Royal for lunch?'

Amelia remembered then that she had told him that she had wanted to be on her own. 'That'll be nice,' she said a little too brightly, and made off purposefully towards a department store across the street where she wandered around feeling lonely. But presently she set about the task of finding presents to take back home, something for Bonny and small gifts for her frrends at St Ansell's. She'd have to buy sweets and chocolates for the nurses in theatre too, and while she was about it, something for the patients. And Tom. . .?

She couldn't see anything she really liked in the store, but there were other shops. She spent the next half hour in an arts and crafts shop, emerging at last with a gaily patterned cardigan for Bonny, a sweater for herself and some exquisite porcelain figures for various of her friends. It was already past the time she had arranged to meet Gideon, so that she had to hurry and arrived a little flustered, to find him standing patiently outside the hotel, and when she apologised he waved it aside with placid good humour, took her parcels from her and ushered her into the restaurant.

'I haven't quite finished,' she explained, 'there's sweets for the ward and the nurses and something for Tom.'

Over the meal they discussed the afternoon. 'I had wondered,' said Gideon casually, 'if you would care to take a trip in the cable car to the top of the mountain just across the river—there's a splendid view of Tromso—but if you haven't finished your shopping. . .?'

'The sweets won't take a minute to buy.' Amelia had quite forgotten for the moment that she had made up her mind not to like him. 'And if I could find a tobacconist I thought I'd buy Tom a pipe. I'm not sure what to buy, though.'

'In that case perhaps I could be of some help? There's a good shop just across the street and a confectioner's a little further down.'

'Would we have time to go to the cathedral?'

He watched her idly while she chose an elaborate creamy pudding from the trolley. 'Plenty of time—we can have a taxi.'

They spent a little time buying chocolates, two large boxes which Gideon obligingly added to his other parcels, and then went into a neighbouring tobacconist, where with his tactful help, Amelia chose a pipe for Tom. Getting into the taxi again, he said: 'We've three hours, so we'll keep this taxi, and he can drive us to the airport.' It seemed a sensible arrangement although a bit extravagant, but Amelia was beginning to enjoy herself. Gideon was surprisingly good company.

They crossed the bridge over the fjord and

went into the hilly suburbs on the further side, where charming wooden houses lined pleasant tree-lined roads. The trees were bare now, of course, but all the same it looked cosy. Amelia would have liked to have lingered there when they got out of the taxi, but the doctor, after a brief conversation with the driver, marched her into the small building at the bottom of the mountain, bought their tickets and bustled her into the cable car.

She didn't much enjoy the trip, it was almost perpendicular and alarmingly lonely, but she obediently looked at the view and once at the top, stepped on to the balcony into the icy wind and gazed obediently at the various features of Tromso, spread out below like a map. Apparently Gideon didn't mind heights; he walked her from one side to the other, anxious for her to miss nothing, and she was beginning to feel decidedly queasy when he observed that if they were to visit the cathedral they should go back. In the cable car she sat with her eyes shut, not daring to look out as they dropped at what seemed a terrifying speed to the bottom of the mountain once more. What was more, she couldn't have cared less if Gideon noticed or not.

But he did. A large arm was suddenly flung across her shoulders. 'My dear girl, you didn't like it! What a fool I am—I should have asked you. I'm so sorry.'

She opened her eyes briefly to look at him.

'It's quite all right—I really did want to go—
everyone does, you know, and so I just had
to. Only I'm a bit of a coward.'

The arm tightened comfortingly. 'Close
your eyes again, we're almost there. Would
you rather go to the airport?'

'No, no, of course not, I'll be perfectly all
right once I'm on the ground. So silly of
me—I'm sorry.'

'You need never say you're sorry to me,
Amelia.' His voice was kindly and quite
impersonal.

He spoke to the driver again and despite
her protests they stopped at a small hotel
before they reached the cathedral, and
Gideon took her inside and at the bar made
her drink some brandy. It made her feel much
better, but a little lightheaded too. 'I'm really
not in a fit state to visit a cathedral,' she
pointed out as they went through its massive
door. He didn't say anything, only took her
arm as they went slowly inside. It was very
quiet and dimly lighted, its pointed roof rising
sharply high above them, magnificent in its
simplicity. Just like a triangle, thought
Amelia, and exactly right for its surroundings. 'Like a mountain,' she said out loud.

'Yes—splendid, isn't it?' observed
Gideon quietly. 'I'm glad we had time to see
it. Now we must go, I'm afraid.'

The flight back seemed short and there was
nothing to see now; the night had enclosed

them completely. They drank the coffee the stewardess brought them and talked about nothing much, nor did they have much to say as they drove back to the hotel from the airport, but once inside again in its warm foyer, Amelia thanked her companion for her day. 'And if you'll let me know my share of the expenses,' she finished a little stiffly.

'My pleasure, Amelia.' His smile caused her to remind herself quite sharply that she didn't like him.

Dinner was a cheerful meal and very talkative, for the American who had spent the day with her father joined them and recounted at some length the various successes and excitements of the trip. Amelia found him garrulous and hoped he wasn't going to be invited to spend the next day with them as well, but she need not have worried. The doctor, although at his most charming, made no such suggestion to their guest and when he had gone later that evening he made the suggestion that they should try a narrow little river running into the Alta above the village. 'I'm told that the weather is going to break within the next day or so, so we might as well make the most of it now,' he added, so that Amelia said quickly: 'Oh, I'm sorry, I shouldn't have taken you from fishing today. What a waste!'

He turned a lazy eye on her. 'Not a waste, Amelia, I enjoyed myself too.'

There was no reason why she should blush

at this prosaic remark, but she did, covering it by becoming very brisk about the morning, and the moment they had decided on the time they wanted to leave, she bade them good-night and went to bed, where she curled up against the pillows, writing a letter to Tom.

The weather held all the next day, although by early evening the wind was icy and the cold bit into their bones, but that didn't stop them planning another day's outing, and after that, a final one. It began to snow while they were at dinner and Gideon suggested that they should fly back immediately after the next two days.

'What about the car?' asked Amelia.

'Oh, that's all arranged. I've got someone to drive it down to Bergen; they'll just about manage it before the roads close. I'll see about a flight and arrange about the boat at Trondheim, if you will allow me?'

Mr Crosbie, glad not to have to arrange things for himself, agreed readily and Amelia, perforce, followed suit, but when they were alone she asked:

'Father, who on earth is going to drive the car all that way? It'll take days!'

'One of the men at the garage, my dear— you may be sure that Gideon will make it well worth his while—he'll fly back, of course. Don't worry about it.' He patted her hand. 'What good fortune that we met up with Gideon, Amelia. This holiday has been twice as enjoyable, I don't know when I've enjoyed myself as much. I like the man, too. . .' He caught her eye and added feebly: 'Well, of course, that doesn't reflect upon Tom. . .'

'Of course not, Father.' Her voice rose a little. 'And I don't know when I've disliked a man so much.'

She was instantly sorry she had said it, especially as it wasn't true. She met her father's astonished stare and added hastily: 'Oh, I didn't mean that—I have no idea why I said it.' She sounded bewildered. 'I wish Tom were here.' Her father didn't answer and she went on briskly: 'It ought to be fun, going by boat. What happens when we get to Bergen?'

'We take the early morning plane to Amsterdam after a good night's sleep at the Norge.' The doctor's quiet voice from behind her sent the colour into her cheeks again and she swung round to face him; perhaps he'd been listening. . .?

He couldn't have; his lazy eyes were almost hidden beneath their lids, his smile was wholly friendly.

'Oh,' she smiled back uncertainly, the relief on her face there for anyone to see, 'I was just saying it should be fun on board.'

'Very likely. There won't be many passengers at this time of year, not on the long trips, though there should be plenty going from one stop to the next. The scenery should be worth seeing, though.'

Amelia only stayed a few minutes after that, long enough to hear the plans for their last day—fishing, of course. She felt that she never wanted to see another salmon or cod for the rest of her days.

It seemed as though the winter had slipped in overnight and taken over. As they set out the sky was clear, but it had been snowing and the wind bit into their faces; all the same it was extraordinarily exhilarating. Amelia, her cheeks red with cold, set about making coffee just as soon as they were on their way. The water of the fjord was decidedly choppy, but that was something that didn't worry her in the least. But despite the wintry day the men agreed at the end of it that they had never had a better catch and she, stamping warmth into her feet, found herself agreeing; it had been exciting and dramatic in such awe-inspiring surroundings, but it had been lighthearted too and somehow soothing. The vague doubts and uncertainties which had been crowding into the back of her mind had been put in their place under the overpowering might of the mountains. They had an uproarious evening, with her father in fine form, and afterwards a kind of farewell party with the other guests. A good thing they weren't flying out until the early afternoon, thought Amelia, going sleepily to bed.

The flight seemed brief, there was so much to see whenever there was a break in the clouds below them and when they reached Trondheim the sun was shining, making the light fall of snow sparkle and the houses look like scenes on a Christmas card. There was still time to visit the Nidaros Cathedral too before returning to the Britannia Hotel for dinner. Amelia, who had wanted to think over her day before she slept, was asleep the moment her head touched the pillow.

There were only a handful of passengers going on board when they got to the dock the next morning. Unlike the previous day, it was cold and grey and almost dark, and Amelia, who had had nothing but a cup of tea when she got up, was relieved to hear that breakfast would be served almost at once.

She went straight to her cabin, unpacked the few things she would need and joined the men on deck. 'I'd like to see us go,' she said hopefully, and hung over the rails as far as she could in order to watch the mail being taken on board followed by box after box of cod. There were last-minute passengers coming on board too, people shouting to each other and the captain, a brisk bearded figure, walking up and down the dock, apparently oblivious of the fact that his ship was on the point of sailing.

'How awful if he got left behind,' remarked Amelia, and earned a: 'Don't be

ridiculous, my dear,' from her father, and a
look from the doctor which she didn't see—
tender and mocking and amused.

The ship's siren sounded, and the captain
came aboard with much the same air of a
man entering the driving seat of his car. A
moment later the ship sidled away from the
dock and within minutes was well into
the fjord.

They watched Trondheim slip away into
the grey morning and Amelia shivered in the
cold. Gideon flung an absentminded arm
round her and she was glad of its warmth
and comfort, although why she should need
comforting, she didn't know.

'A pity we had no more time to see
Trondheim,' said Gideon. 'It's a fine city—
another time, perhaps.' Before she could tell
him that there wasn't likely to be another
time, not for the three of them together, at
any rate, the gong went for breakfast.

Amelia, quite famished, what with cold
and excitement and getting up early, wandered round the long table with its display
of herrings in sauce, cheese, cold meat, any
number of varieties of bread and nicest of all,
a great bowl of porridge, helped herself and
sat down at the table they had been given.
There weren't many passengers: two
Americans sampling the round trip for
a travel agency in New York, several
Norwegians, most of them businessmen

calling for one reason or another at the smaller towns and villages en route, and a handful of keen fishermen like themselves.

After the meal everyone found their way to the saloon on the deck above, there to admire the view, exchange gossip about their holidays and in the case of the sportsmen, tell each other fishy stories. Amelia saw very little of either her father or the doctor, but the Americans, delighted to find someone who listened well, kept her a captive audience until the gong went for lunch when she found that a young Norwegian on his way back to Bergen from Trondheim had joined them at table, so that the conversation was general. It was like that for the rest of the day and the following morning too, and she told herself that it was rather nice not to have Gideon's constant companionship. All the same she felt strangely lonely.

CHAPTER FOUR

THERE wasn't time to do much in Bergen, although when they had landed after lunch and settled in at the Norge, Gideon took Amelia to the Bryggens Museum, where they wandered round for an hour examining the runic inscriptions, ceramics and jewellery while he explained the cultural habits of the twelfth century to her. He seemed to know a great deal about it; probably he was a clever man, hiding his learning under a casual manner. They had tea in Reimers Tea-Room and then crossed the square to the hotel. A very pleasant afternoon, decided Amelia, changing for the evening into the jersey dress. Perhaps dinner would be fun, and they might dance afterwards. . .

It didn't turn out like that, though. When she got down to the bar it was to find her father and Gideon deep in conversation with the two Americans who had been on the ship, an English couple who were staying in Bergen on their way to Oslo and two young-ish Norwegians. It was Gideon who suggested that they should dine together and presently they all sat down together at one large table, and when someone suggested dancing, Amelia was annoyed to see him ask the American girl to dance. Not that she lacked partners; and she was very glad, when Gideon did at length come across to ask her to dance—probably out of good manners, she thought waspishly—that she was able to skip away, with a few seconds to spare, with one of the Norwegians.

She was coolly friendly in the morning. It was a pity that what with getting themselves to the airport and boarding the plane for Schiphol, there was little opportunity for Gideon to notice it. And once on board they were kept busy, drinking coffee, eating the sandwiches they were offered, reading the newspapers, the men, one on each side of her, engrossed themselves in the sport news, exchanging casual comments across her, occasionally politely including her in them. She was very glad when Gideon pointed out the flat lands of Holland below them.

'I don't even know exactly where you live,' she told him coldly.

'No? Between Amsterdam and Utrecht, in a small village beside a lake. Very quiet and peaceful, although it's close to the motorway. It's flat too, quite different from Norway. I hope you will like it.'

'How do we get there?'

'Jorrit will have brought a car to meet the plane. He's my general factotum.' He didn't add anything, although she was dying of curiosity. Presently, she reminded herself, she would see everything for herself.

They went through the airport with tolerable speed and were met in the enormous reception hall by a very tall, thin man of middle age with a face so composed Amelia wondered if he ever smiled or frowned. He did indeed smile when he saw the doctor, bowed his head to her and her father and without further preamble led the way outside, where they had to wait a minute while the porter caught up with them.

'This is Jorrit,' Gideon introduced the man, 'he speaks English, by the way. He has been in the family for a very long time.' He smiled at Jorrit, whose calm was once more broken by a brief smile. 'He'll drive the estate car with the luggage and we'll go on ahead.'

He spoke again to Jorrit, who nodded and turned to the porter and Gideon led the way to where an Aston Martin Lagonda stood. As he unlocked its door Mr Crosbie said enthusiastically: 'I say, this is nice—didn't expect to see one here, though—they're hard enough to get at home.'

And expensive enough, added Amelia silently, getting into the back and leaving her father to get in beside the doctor. But it was a lovely car; she sat listening to the men discussing its teething troubles and watching the scenery. It was indeed different from Norway, and presently Gideon began to point out one or two things of interest. They had cut across to join the motorway leading from Amsterdam to Utrecht. The road ran through the southern suburb of Amstelveen, but presently, at the roundabout a few miles further on, he turned south, sending the car along the road at a fine pace, so that Amelia had no time to see a great deal anyway. Indeed, she was more interested in watching Gideon. He drove well, as though he and the big car were all of one piece, and although the motorway was crowded, he kept up his speed, weaving easily in and out of the lanes. At the next roundabout he turned off, following a flyover away from the main stream and after a mile or so, turned off again, this time into a country road, rather cold and lonely in the quiet wintry countryside, but only briefly, for suddenly there was water on either side of them. 'Loenenveensche Plas,' observed Gideon, 'it runs south almost to Utrecht. Hilversum is quite close, but we turn down the other side, there are only small villages along the bank. My home is between two of them.'

Amelia had expected a comfortable house, even a fair sized one, for the doctor was obviously a man living in comfortable circumstances, but she wasn't quite prepared for the grandeur of the wrought iron gates, open between high stone gate posts crowned by mythical stone animals. And she certainly wasn't prepared for the sight which met her eyes as they rounded a curve in the drive. It wasn't a house at all, but a castle—a small one, it was true, but there it stood, with a pepperpot turret on one side of its massive front door and its ancient red brick walls rising from what must at one time have been the moat.

'Well, I never!' exclaimed Amelia in astonishment. 'What a darling place!' It struck her forcibly that she had no idea of the doctor's domestic arrangements. Did he live with his parents. Surely not by himself?

Apparently he did, for he said almost apologetically: 'Yes, it is rather. It was built for a family, of course, not for a bachelor.'

Amelia was getting out of the car and looking about her. Double steps led to the entrance and she longed to see inside, a wish granted almost immediately as the door was opened by a small round lady who stood back to allow her to see beyond into a softly lit hall. 'Jorrit's wife,' observed Gideon as he led the way up the steps, 'my housekeeper too.' He gave the small creature a great hug and introduced her as Tyske and she shook hands, beaming from a round jolly face as they went inside.

The hall was square with a carved wooden staircase climbing up one wall to a gallery above, and furnished with several very large antique chairs, a couple of marble-topped wall tables and some fine silk rugs on its black and white marble floor. The walls were panelled in the same dark wood as the stairs and hung with a number of portraits, presumably of the doctor's forebears. Amelia had no chance to inspect them, for they were led at once into a large room with a very large bow window at one end and an equally large fireplace at the other. The window was draped with curtains of ruby velvet tied back with cords and the carpet was of the same colour, a nice foil to the faded colours of the tapestry covered chairs. There were two very large sofas too, drawn up on each side of the blazing fire in the hearth, its copper hood glistening in the flames. The walls, unlike the hall, were papered in a silk damask of a rich cream and almost covered by still more portraits. The doctor, Amelia reflected, must either have an enormous family or an ancestry which went back several hundred years. She took the seat offered her with composure, liking her surroundings but not unduly cowed by them; her own home, although smaller, was just as splendidly furnished and it seemed likely that her ancestors, man for man and woman for woman, would equal his.

Gideon made no observations about his home and probably wouldn't have done so, but Mr Crosbie, his attention drawn to a glass-fronted cabinet against one wall, remarked with some pleasure that he had a very similar pair of *cassolettes* in his own home. 'The enamel covers are by Craft, I daresay,' he observed. 'Made by Boulton, and frankly hideous. At least I think so.'

Gideon went to stand by him. 'I couldn't agree more. I like something simpler, myself; this silver-gilt side table ewer—it's French and mid-eighteenth century. I haven't much English stuff, though—a coffee-pot, George II, I believe, which an ancestress brought over with her as part of her dowry, and which I use when I'm home, and a silver sugar box. That came with her too. That was a splendid period for silversmiths in England. I must envy you that.'

Mr Crosbie beamed at him. 'My dear chap, you may well do so. I've some splendid pieces at home—you really must pay us a visit some time and I'll show you the lot.'

'I shall enjoy that.' He turned to look at Amelia. 'I'm sure you'd like to go to your room; Tyske will bring tea in about ten minutes if that suits you.'

He pulled on a faded bell rope and a young girl with red cheeks and very blue eyes answered it. 'This is Mien, one of the house-maids, she'll take you upstairs.' He said something to the girl, who smiled and nodded and waited by the door and when Amelia had joined her, led the way up the staircase and along the gallery and down a little passage, up three steps and then opened a very solid door. The room was in the turret, its rounded side lighted by four narrow windows. There was a bright fire burning in a small steel grate in the opposite wall casting a warm glow on the plain white walls. The bed was a small canopied one, hung with toile de Jouy in pink and white, and the curtains were of the same material and the same pink was used for the silk quilt on the bed. There was a spindle-legged table with a triple mirror under the windows and a high-backed armchair. It was a very pretty room, and Amelia, examining it with interest, wished she were staying more than one night in it.

She remarked upon it when she went downstairs and Gideon said carelessly: 'It is rather charming, isn't it? It was my youngest sister's until she married.'

'How many sisters have you?' She hadn't thought of him as having a family and he had never mentioned them.

'Three, all younger than I and all married. I have a young brother too, Reinier, he's studying medicine at Utrecht.' He smiled lazily at her. 'My mother lives outside Soest, which isn't far away from here; she didn't want to live here after my father died.'

Amelia longed to ask questions, but she didn't dare, not in the face of his bland offer of information—indeed, she went a little red because she had been inquisitive and he had known it. Instead, she seated herself by the rosewood tea table and poured tea for them all, and listened to him and her father discussing their holiday. Somehow it all seemed a long way away.

They dined presently in a richly sombre room with a circular table to seat a dozen or more and a vast sideboard. It was restful too, its thick carpet a silver grey to offset the yew of the furniture, its curtains dark olive green velvet, matching the upholstery of the chairs. Amelia wished heartily that she had rather more variety to her wardrobe. Her silk blouse with its little waistcoat and skirt were all very well, but they hardly did justice to her surroundings.

They sat round the fire after a dinner which would have earned itself at least four stars in a glossy magazine, the men with cognac glasses, Amelia contenting herself with coffee, and presently she excused herself on the pretext that she was very tired, and went upstairs to her pretty room.

She wasn't tired at all, she had never felt so wide awake. She toured her room again, admired the bathroom once more, went to look out of the windows and was surprised to see Gideon with two long-haired Alsatians, walking below. He looked up as he passed and waved. She half lifted her hand to wave back and then thought better of it; the unspoken thought that Tom might not like it crossed her mind as she turned away and let the curtains fall.

Winter had followed hard on their heels, it seemed. Amelia woke early and nipped from her warm bed to pull back the curtains and enjoy the view. The sun was beginning to warm the sky, although it still wasn't visible, turning the cold blue to a pale pink which in turn lent colour to the frost-covered world. She stood entranced until a knock on the door sent her flying back to bed.

It was her morning tea, and when the maid had gone Amelia got out of bed again, put on her dressing gown and went back to the window, curling up on the window seat with her cup in her hand. The outside world was too good to miss and tomorrow she would be in London and see nothing but grey streets and rows of houses. And Tom, of course, she reminded herself. She was enjoying her second cup when Gideon with his two dogs came into her view, and this time, carried away by some impulse she didn't try to understand, she opened the casement and called good morning.

He stopped and looked up. 'Good morning, Amelia. Put on some clothes and come down. A walk'll do you good. You can have five minutes.'

She managed it somehow, bundled into slacks and a sweater and her quilted jacket on top. She cleaned her teeth, but there was no time for her hair or face; the latter was rosy with sleep and her head a dark tangled curtain as she raced downstairs to meet him.

His quiet: 'Lord, what a lovely girl you are, Amelia,' brought her up short. She had wanted to be with him, so much that she hadn't cared what she looked like, and the sudden knowledge of that shocked her into a frozen silence. She stood in front of him, her face a stiff little mask of bewilderment and embarrassment.

He studied her slowly, his head on one side. 'Oh, dear—why have you gone all frosty?' he wanted to know, 'just when I thought. . .well, never mind what I thought. You remind me of a winter's frost waiting for a silver thaw, Amelia.'

'A silver thaw? What's that?'

'Something only to be found in Oregon, I believe; after a frost when the thaw sets in, it turns to silver in the warmth of the sun. It is reputed to be beautiful, just as you are beautiful—only you haven't found the right warmth to thaw you yet, have you, my dear?'

She whispered: 'You mustn't say things like that. Tom. . .'

Gideon smiled mockingly at her, took her arm and whistled to the dogs. 'Do you like dogs? I imagine so. This is Nel and this one is Prince—they're still quite young. I had their mother for years. They love this weather.'

Amelia was beginning to feel normal again in the light of his casual friendliness. 'It's a lovely day and Holland is so pretty   I somehow thought of it as quite flat with no trees at all. It's very rural, isn't it?'

'For a few miles each way, yes.' He took her across the back of the castle and along a flagged path leading to a wicket gate which he opened. It led to a water meadow, striped with narrow canals, iced over and on the further side, a line of trees.

'Is this your field?' asked Amelia, determined to make normal conversation.

'Yes, and the next one too, down as far as the river. I keep a boat there, for it's no distance to the Loosdrechtse Plassen—they're a series of lakes.' He talked on, putting her at her ease, so that by the time they reached the house again she was almost ready to forget her awkward moment and went happily indoors to have a shower and dress for breakfast.

Her father joined them at breakfast and they all three walked across the fields to take a look at the river, making its sedate way between the frosty meadows. It was on the way back that Mr Crosbie remembered that he hadn't told Badger the exact time of their arrival and went on ahead to telephone him, leaving Gideon to show Amelia round the hot house. She was admiring a magnificent display of azaleas when he asked suddenly:

'You intend marrying Tom soon?'

She took a quick look at his face and saw that he was wearing a bland look again and for some reason she felt wary of it. 'I did tell you, at least I think I did—we're going to wait until he's well established.'

'Of course, I'd forgotten—stupid of me.' His voice was very smooth. 'I imagined that perhaps your week together. . .?'

He left the question hanging in the air.

'Made no difference at all,' she snapped. She hadn't meant to say that, and she had no idea why she had. She was so vexed with herself that she could have cried.

He had strolled to the other side of the bench so that he could see her face and unless she turned her back on him there was no way of preventing him from doing it. 'Why not marry me?' he asked her quietly.

Amelia jerked her head up in amazement, the whole of her suddenly intent on getting the conversation back on to a rational footing. 'Why on earth should I want marry you?' she asked haughtily.

He said mildly: 'Oh, I don't know—I've a large and comfortable home to offer you.'

'I already have a large and comfortable home, thank you.'

'So much the better—you would have two. And think of the children.'

She gasped: 'I haven't got any children!'

He answered her with an amused patience

which made her grit her splendid teeth. 'Of course not, dear girl; that takes time, but a family of, say, three would need room in which to grow, don't you agree? What could be a pleasanter childhood for them? And when we're old and helpless. . .'

He was joking, and she didn't know whether to be sorry or glad about it. Her fierce frown smoothed itself and she chuckled. 'You're absurd! You may get old, but you'll never be helpless.'

'Ah, now that's a sound argument. I shall be able to look after you and cherish you until my last breath.'

He was smiling, but he was staring at her too, with a look in his eyes which set her heart thumping, stilling the chuckle. Surely it was a joke?

'I'm going to marry Tom,' she said in a voice which try as she might held a note of uncertainty.

The heavy lids had dropped over his eyes once again, and his voice was placid.

'Ah, well, there was no harm in trying,' he observed. 'Now, you really must look at the grapes—we're very proud of them. Through this door.'

There was a very thin, very old man bending over a tray of seedlings in the neighbouring hothouse. He straightened up slowly as they approached and Gideon went to peer at the contents of the tray. 'This is Jaap, he's

eighty-one and has no intention of retiring —
he's a wizard with everything that grows.'

Amelia murmured a reply. She was feeling
quite out of her depth, uncertain of Gideon
and of herself, and now here he was expecting
her to enthuse about a box of seeds! But the
old man was a dear, his leathery face lighted
by the bluest eyes she had ever seen. He
smiled at her with the innocence of a child
and she found herself smiling back; in the
end she carried on quite a long conversation
with him with Gideon standing between
them, translating.

They went back to the castle presently and
Amelia carried on a highly artificial conversation, repeating herself continuously and
rushing on to another topic whenever there
was a silence of more than a few seconds.
Gideon answered her gravely, his mouth
twitching uncontrollably at its corners. For a
man who had had his proposal of marriage
turned down in no uncertain manner he
looked singularly undisturbed.

They had coffee in a small room which
took up the base of the tower, directly under
her bedroom. It was full of light and the
chintz curtains and covers were cheerful
against its panelled walls. Amelia, sitting by
the fire warming her cold toes, sipped her
delicious coffee and took care not to meet
Gideon's eyes, while she talked animatedly
about nothing in particular. Her father gave

her an odd look once or twice, for she was normally a restful girl, not given to idle chatter.

It was while he was taking them round his home that she asked Gideon where he worked. 'You haven't a surgery here?' she wanted to know.

'No—I've rooms in Utrecht and I go there each day. I have beds in the hospital there, and in Amsterdam, and I go to The Hague.'

She was examining a marquetry cabinet, very ornate, and didn't look at him. 'You specialise?' she persisted.

'Anaesthetics. Don't you find this quite meaningless? All these porcelain plaques and gilt bronze. I long to send it to the attics, but Tyske won't hear of it.'

Mr Crosbie, who had been looking at the pictures, joined them. 'We've something very similar at home, can't stand the thing myself. Nasty showy piece. That's a splendid bit of marquetry on that writing table, though—eighteenth century, isn't it?' He bent to examine it. 'You've some fine pieces here, Gideon. I'd like you to visit us and have a look round our place. We can't boast a castle, though.'

'It sounds delightful.' Gideon's voice was very smooth. 'There's nothing I should like better, but for the immediate future I'm rather heavily booked up.'

'Got plenty of friends, I'll be bound.'

'Well, yes, that among other things.'

Amelia, her ears stretched to hear every word, longed to ask what things. It was a good thing, she told herself, that she was going home that very afternoon and would never set eyes on Gideon again. And if he ever decided to pay them a visit, then she would take good care not to be at home.

They lunched presently, a delicious meal of prawns in aspic, lamb cutlets and tangerine syllabub. Amelia, who usually enjoyed her food, hardly noticed what she ate and the sherry she had had before they sat down, reinforced by a vintage claret, merely served to make her feel hazy and strangely unhappy. Because the holiday was over, she decided silently, and made even greater efforts at bright conversation.

They had their coffee in the drawing room, sitting comfortably by the great hearth, surrounded by all its grandeur, and far too soon for her Jorrit came to say that their suitcases had been put in the car and they should prepare to leave in ten minutes.

Amelia got up at once to go to her room and put on her coat and Gideon got up with her. 'Such a pity I can't drive you myself,' he apologised, 'but I've a couple of patients to see this afternoon. Jorrit will see you safely away, though.'

And a good thing too, thought Amelia as she put on her outdoor things; enough is enough. Quite what she meant by this remark she had no idea, but it comforted her a little and she presented a bright face to the two gentlemen waiting for her in the drawing room. Her father shook hands with Gideon, said all that was polite and went to the door, and she made to follow him. But somehow Gideon got between her and her father, who walked out of the room and shut the door behind him, leaving her standing awkwardly within inches of her host.

'Goodbye, Amelia.' His voice was quiet and unhurried. 'Oh, we shall probably meet again some time, it is, as they say a very small world, but even if we do it is still good-bye. You understand that, don't you?'

She nodded without looking higher than his waistcoat. Unexplained desolation left her hollow, and even if she understood how she felt she couldn't have found the words to tell him.

'Amelia?' His voice was so gentle and compelling that she looked up to meet his steady gaze, and once she had done that she was lost; she was unable to take her eyes away from his face. The thought that she would remember every line of it for the rest of her days crossed her unhappy mind, but she swept it away. 'I'm going to marry Tom, we've known each other for a very long time. I—I met you three weeks ago.'

A little smile touched his mouth. 'Yes, I

hadn't forgotten.' He bent his head before she could move back and kissed her hard and then again, gently this time, then went quickly to the door and opened it for her. She could see her father in the hall, talking to Jorrit and Tyske as she went past him. She didn't say anything—indeed, her throat had closed over with a quite unexpected rush of tears. She swallowed them back, smiled at Tyske and followed Jorrit and her father to the car. It cost her a great effort not to look back as they drove away.

Their flight back was uneventful, and with Badger waiting for them at Heathrow, there was nothing to do but follow the rest of the passengers out of the airport. Amelia walked between her father and Badger and listened to their talk; nice, everyday talk about the plumbers coming to fit a new sink in the flower room and having the sweep and the vicar having 'flu. Badger had asked her if she had enjoyed her holiday and she had said yes, very much, thank you and fallen silent again, just as silent as she had been sitting beside her father in the plane.

Badger was to drive them to St Ansell's first and then go on home with Mr Crosbie. The late afternoon rush hour was just starting and it took some time to cross London; it was a relief when they reached the hospital and she was able to bid her parent and Badger goodbye. 'And I'll let you know when I'm coming home for days off,' she told them. 'I'll phone one evening.'

She kissed her father and he took her hand for a moment. 'You enjoyed your holiday, my dear? You're not tired? You've been very quiet.'

'It was lovely, Father, and thank you very much for taking me. I've been thinking about it all the way home.' Which was true enough.

There was a note from Tom in the porter's lodge. He had duty until midnight so he would see her sometime in the morning; he hoped she'd had a pleasant trip back. She hadn't realised, until she read it, how she had been banking on seeing him that evening. She went over to her room, looking up those of her friends who were off duty, and went down to supper with them, answering their questions with a rather feverish gaiety and avoiding any mention of Gideon; somehow she didn't want to tell anyone about him. Perhaps, she told herself, if she did that, the memory of him would fade. Anyway, when she saw Tom, she would forget all about Gideon; it was a passing episode and had assumed greater proportions than it deserved simply because there had been no one and nothing else of interest while she had been in Norway.

She argued with herself half the night and went down to breakfast a little edgy, which would never do: it was Mr Thomley-Jones' list and from what she had heard his temper had been decidedly nasty since his return from holiday. She decided that she didn't mind if it was; it would give her something to think about.

She was right. She was kept busy all day, licking her team back into shape, adjusting to Mr Thomley-Jones' humours, giving covert assistance to the new surgical houseman who, while quite happy with the simple appendices and hernias, was completely out of his depth when a stabbed man was rushed into theatre and had several hours spent on him while every inch of his gut was scrutinised and if necessary stitched. All in all, it was the kind of day Amelia could have done without, and when at last she got off duty it was to discover that Tom was doing an extra duty because the other registrar had fallen sick. She went to bed early, decidedly peevish.

And the next day was just as bad, work-wise, although this time Tom was free and had left a message for her to meet him that evening. She bathed and changed into the new suit, covered it with the long chunky knitted coat which looked so simple and had cost her a small fortune, and went down to the residents' car park. Tom was waiting for her and because she was still feeling unsettled it annoyed her that he stayed sitting behind the wheel until she was beside him. His hullo was friendly and the kiss he gave her was affectionate, and she was horrified to find herself comparing it with Gideon's kiss. Of course, she told herself hastily, Gideon was probably in the habit of kissing any girl he met, which would account for his expertise.

'Sorry about yesterday,' said Tom, 'but we're a bit shorthanded at the moment. I knew you'd understand. The senior house physician offered to take over, but there are one or two tricky cases and I thought it best to do the duty myself.'

It was on the tip of her tongue to say that he might have handed over for an hour, half an hour even—after all, the other man was qualified and from what she'd heard of him, he was pretty good too. But she had never interfered with Tom's work and she didn't mean to start now. She assured him that she understood and asked where they were going.

He smiled at her. 'That quiet little place off the Brompton Road. I've a great deal to tell you.'

Her heart quickened its beat. The holiday together had decided him, and he was going to marry her soon; she would be able to settle down to being a housewife-cum-theatre-Sister and once they were married she had every intention of persuading him to let her be just a housewife. She agreed happily and sat chatting on and off while he drove to the restaurant.

It wasn't until they had had their soup,

their lemon sole and were half way through their pudding that Tom said suddenly: 'I've got a job!'

Amelia put down her fork. She had been hard put to it to keep a light conversation going, but she had been determined not to ask any questions. She smiled across the table, her eyebrows raised to a question.

'In Australia,' he added.

'*Australia*? So far? When?'

'I go in a month.'

She stared at him stupidly. 'But how can you? Don't you have to give three months' notice?'

'Only a month—you forget I finished my three years' contract several months ago.'

Amelia managed a normal voice. 'What part of Australia?'

'Perth. A marvellous new hospital with unlimited scope. . .' His eyes were shining at the thought.

She said faintly, repeating herself. 'But, Tom, it's so far away. Father. . . Is it for long?'

'Five years.'

She struggled to gather her woolly wits. 'And you accepted without saying a word to me?'

'Well, as a matter of fact, they won't take a married man. But that's O.K.; you can go on working here and at the end of my contract I should most certainly get a consultant's appointment, when we could be married.'

'You mean,' said Amelia slowly, 'that I'm to stay here until it's—it's convenient for us to marry? Tom, in five years I'll be thirty-two! We've been engaged ages already.' She gulped back tears and steadied her voice with some effort. 'Look, Tom, don't I mean anything to you? Don't you love me? So much that you'd give up everything for me if I asked?' The words, so well remembered, tumbled out of her mouth. 'Cherish me until your last breath?'

Tom was looking at her in utter amazement, his nice face a mixture of embarrassment and dismay. 'My dear Amelia, what are you waffling on about? That's silly girl's talk. I thought better of you; you're a sensible young woman.'

She whispered fiercely: 'I'm not, I'm not—and soon I won't be young any more. Oh, Tom, what about children and making a home together and having a dog and a cat and going out for picnics on Sundays. . .'

His embarrassment was tinged with impatience now. 'Look, dear, you've had a surprise. Let's go back to St Ansell's and you have a good night's sleep and in the morning you'll see it in a rational light.'

She tried just once more. 'Tom, won't you look for a job in England? For my sake?'

He smiled kindly. 'You know how important my work is to me.'

'More important than I am?'

He considered that carefully. 'That's hard to answer, but in a way, if I must be honest—yes, it is.'

There really wasn't any more to say, not just then. 'Well, let's go back,' she said quietly.

They drove through the busy streets while Tom told her of his plans, and she wasn't in any of them, she noted sadly, but then she couldn't expect to be, not for five years. He parked the car at the back of the hospital and they went in through a side door and because there were a good many people about he didn't do more than pat her on the shoulder and tell her, once again, to have a good night's sleep.

Amelia said goodnight very quietly because now wasn't the time to talk; she had to marshal her thoughts and her arguments first, and she could do that during the night.

CHAPTER FIVE

THE night didn't prove long enough. Amelia was heavy-eyed through lack of sleep when she went down to breakfast and was hard put to it to make a joking reply when someone at her table remarked that she looked as though she had been quarrelling with Tom all night. 'There's a rumour going round that he's got himself a super job in Australia—is it true, Amelia?'

She answered that yes, it was, with composure, and contrived to give a vague answer to the rain of questions as to her own future. Everyone seemed to take it for granted that she and Tom would marry before he left, or if not that, then she would go with him and get married when they arrived.

'Well, nothing's settled yet,' she told them evasively. 'We've not really had the time to talk it over. . .'

'That means you'll get married in a rush here or in jeans and a straw hat in some awful bush station or whatever,' moaned Jean Hawkins, one of her closest friends and Sister on Men's Medical, 'and I did so want to be a bridesmaid!'

Amelia managed a goodnatured laugh. 'Go

on with you, you know you'd rather be the bride, any day,' a remark which set the table laughing so that for the moment they forgot to ask her any more questions.

It was a mercy that Mr Godwin was operating that morning. He worked his way placidly through a lengthy list, talking in his calm way, not seeming to notice her brief replies, making sure that everyone stopped for coffee during the morning and never turning a hair when one of the nurses slipped and dropped a small tray of instruments. Amelia, whose nerves were stretched like taut elastic, had a hard job not to turn on the hapless girl and tear her in pieces; as it was she said woodenly: 'Pick up everything, Nurse, get them washed and autoclaved and then fetch me the spare set from the end cupboard.' She couldn't stop herself saying sharply: 'And be quick, please!'

Everyone looked at her because she was never anything but calm and good-tempered in theatre, but no one said anything.

She didn't go down to her dinner but had a sandwich in the office, giving the excuse that there was a gynae list starting at half past one and she really hadn't the time. That she had two perfectly adequate staff nurses on duty to lay up seemed to have escaped her notice; she went into the little room and shut the door and tried to decide when she would see Tom again and what she would say to him when she did.

By the time she went off duty at five o'clock she was quite decided. She had thought out all the rational things to say and she was going to ask him just once more if he would give up the new job in favour of something nearer home. And she had got over the shock of it now; she could think clearly once more and she had no intention of weeping or anything silly like that.

It was a pity that Tom rang her just before she left the theatre to say that his chief had asked him to dinner so that he could hear all about the new post. 'When are you off tomorrow?' asked Tom cheerfully.

'I'm on at ten o'clock.'

'Oh, lord, that means you won't be available until the evening—let's meet for a drink then? How about the Lamb and Garter? I'll wait for you by the porter's lodge—about eight o'clock. See you then.'

He hadn't asked her if she had slept, or how she felt, he hadn't mentioned the new job. Her faint hope that he might have had second thoughts about it faded away. She sat looking at the phone, wishing that there was someone she could talk to about it. Perhaps she was being selfish and unreasonable, but if Tom could take a momentous decision like that without saying a word to her wasn't that a bad augury for the future? And was she so unreasonable to mind being left behind for five years? She found herself wishing that Gideon was there, sitting opposite her, listening to all that she had to say and never mind if he mocked her a little or made unanswerable remarks. At least he would listen and tell her what to do.

She got to her feet and left the theatre, calling goodnight to the staff nurse as she went. The evening stretched aimlessly before her and if she went to the sitting room she would be bombarded with questions. 'I'll have a headache,' she muttered, 'and go to bed early.'

As it turned out she slept, for she was very tired and when she woke in the morning everything seemed all right. She would be able to talk Tom round; he could find another job easily enough. He was a good doctor and if only he would accept a loan from her father he could buy a partnership and they could settle down and live happily. And forget Gideon, said a tiny voice somewhere in the back of her head. She brushed it aside; his memory was only persistent because he had said one or two strange things to her—he had been joking, of course, when he had suggested that she should marry him. It wasn't quite as easy to brush aside the memory of his kiss, because it had disturbed her greatly, but once she and Tom were married, she would forget the whole episode.

She went through a busy day quite happily, hurried over her supper and changed into one of her pretty dresses and the thick knit coat. She looked enchanting as she flew down the stairs and through the hospital; her cheeks glowed and her eyes sparkled and even Tom's quiet: 'Hullo, Amelia, you look a bit het up,' didn't make any difference. She took his arm although he didn't really like her to and they went out of the hospital gates and down the road for a little way to the Lamb and Garter. The bar was packed, but they found a table jammed up against a wall and sat down and Tom went to get their drinks—a pint of bitter for him and a sherry for Amelia, which was what they always had. She found herself wishing that he would have come back with two champagne cocktails or even whisky, just by way of a change, although she didn't care for whisky at all and champagne cocktails, in her experience, were reserved for weddings and christenings and engagement parties.

'Did you have a nice evening?' she asked him as he sat down beside her.

'Oh, splendid. Old Coles'—his chief—'was out in Perth himself about ten years ago; he was able to give me a lot of tips.'

'You're really going, then?' She tried to make her voice bright.

'Well, of course I am—I told you so the other evening. We had it all arranged. . .'

'No,' she corrected him quietly, 'you mean *you* had it all arranged. I had no say in the matter, Tom.'

He looked at her uneasily. 'Look here, Amelia, let's get this settled once and for all. This is a super job and I intend to take it. . .'

'For five years—five years, Tom, that's ages! In that time you could meet another girl you wanted to marry, I might meet another man, or I'll grow into a bachelor girl and not want to marry you after all.'

He asked patiently: 'So what do you suggest?'

'Oh, Tom, you know already!' Her eager voice shook a little; so much depended on his answer. 'If you would get a partnership or another registrar's post at a good hospital somewhere in England, so we could get married. I'll go on working if you really want me to. . .'

It wasn't going to be any good; her voice faltered and died. For something to do she took a sip of sherry and then recklessly tossed off the lot; she was going to need it.

Tom put down his tankard. He said in his reasonable way: 'Amelia, nothing is going to make me change my mind, you must try and understand —this is important to me.'

'More important than I am.' She wanted to cry, but it would never do to make a fool of herself in the Lamb and Garter. 'Tom, do you mind if we go?'

'We've only just got here.'

She stared at him for a long moment. He expected her to sit there until he had finished his beer; he didn't mind that he was breaking her heart. She slid the ring off her third finger and laid it on the table beside him and got to her feet. She had slipped through the crowded bar and was out of the door before Tom grasped what she had done. It took her no time at all to reach the hospital; within ten minutes she had gained her room, torn off her clothes and run a bath. If she was going to have a good cry she might as well be warm while she was having it.

She didn't see Tom at all during the next day, which was just as well, for she was in no fit state to talk to him and the following day she had, fortunately, her two days off.

She drove herself home after being on duty all day and arrived late in the evening to be fussed over by Badger and Bonny. Her father was out to dinner, they told her as Badger took her case, poured her a sherry and assured her that Bonny would have a tasty little supper ready for her within half an hour. It was soothing to be looked after with so much affection. It also made her feel tearful again, so she drank another glass of sherry, ate her supper because otherwise Bonny would want to know why she hadn't, and then settled by the fire to await her father's return.

He was late, so late in fact that Amelia was

dozing when he came into the room and only woke to the sound of his efforts to be quiet and not disturb her.

As soon as he saw that she was awake he bent to kiss her. 'Hullo, my dear, nice to see you, so soon too—if I'd known you were coming I'd have cried off my dinner party. I thought you said you'd not be home until next week.'

She sat up, pushing her hair away from her face. 'I did, Father, only something's happened. Tom and I– we're not going to get married.'

Her father leant forward and patted her hand. 'My dear, I'm sorry, but not surprised.'

'Oh, aren't you? He's got a job in Australia, rather a special one in Perth, only they don't want a married man, so he he accepted a contract for five years and I was supposed to stay here until he got another job.'

'Still working, I take it?'

'Oh, yes.' Two tears trickled down her cheeks and she wiped them away impatiently. 'Father, am I being very selfish? I just can't face five years of theatre and living like a nun and suppose he finds someone else out there? What would I do?'

'You did quite right, Amelia. Five years is a hazard in such circumstances. There aren't many men who would be prepared. . .' He paused. 'No, that's not quite true, once in a lifetime one meets a man and a woman who are willing to wait for the whole of their lives, but that's because they love each other so deeply that nothing else really counts. But that's not you and Tom, my dear.'

Amelia said indignantly: 'Father, I'm broken-hearted—I don't know what I'm going to do.'

'Yes, of course you are, just for the time, and never mind about worrying what you're going to do. Drift, my dear, drift, meet each day as it comes, go out, make yourself take an interest in life.' He sighed. 'I only wish your mother were here, Amelia, she would know exactly how to say what I'm trying to.'

'Would she?' Amelia smiled a little. Her mother had died when she was still quite a little girl, but she hadn't forgotten her. 'But she didn't know, did she? I mean, she met you and lived happily ever after.'

'My dear child, your mother and I didn't see each other for three years during the war. Three years is a long time, especially when you've only been married for a couple of weeks. But I'll tell you something—it made no difference to us, you see we loved each other so much, just to know that the other was somewhere on earth was enough.' He went across to the side table and poured himself a whisky and after a moment, poured one for Amelia too. 'I hope that one day you'll understand what I mean.'

'I don't think I ever want to get married,' declared Amelia, accepting the whisky and pulling a face as she sipped it.

'A very proper sentiment for the moment, my dear. When does Tom go?'

'Quite soon in a week or so.'

'The quicker the better. It will be a good deal easier for you when he has gone. We'll have to fill in your days for you. Which reminds me, we've received an invitation to your cousin Barbara's wedding St George's, Hanover Square, in three weeks' time. Your aunt is pulling out all the stops, I understand. We'll have to go, of course. Buy yourself a new outfit, Amelia, we mustn't let the side down.'

It was a happy remark, for it served to distract Amelia from her misery, even for a short time. She and Barbara disliked each other intensely; they had been made to play together as children while their nannies looked on under the impression that they liked each other's company, unaware that when they weren't looking Barbara, a spoilt brat if ever there was one, amused herself by pinching Amelia, whose only reason for not pinching back was the fact that she was four years older and it wouldn't be sporting. She had had her small triumphs since those days, though. She was a great deal more popular than Barbara and for several years went out and about a good deal. It wasn't until she met

Tom that she dropped out of her circle of friends. And she got engaged, much to Barbara's annoyance and now the wretched girl had got engaged herself and managed an early wedding. Amelia, forgetting Tom for a few minutes, took pleasure in planning the sort of outfit which would attract attention, purely on the grounds of annoying her cousin.

But it didn't last long. She finished her whisky, said goodnight to her father and went off to bed.

A month had seemed such a long time when Tom had told her he was going, but it proved to be otherwise. A good thing in a way, because she was kept busy in theatre and had little or no opportunity of seeing him. Indeed, it had been awkward to say the least when she encountered him on her way off duty after she got back from her days off, but after exchanging a stiff good evening Tom had retraced his steps and walked along the corridors with her.

'There's no reason why we shouldn't be friends,' he pointed out. 'In this modern age I hope we've learnt to be reasonable.'

Amelia had never felt less reasonable. 'There doesn't seem much point,' she began.

'Surely a meal together somewhere wouldn't hurt either of us? There's a lot I want to tell you about this job.'

She felt astonishment. That Tom actually

expected her to adopt the role of old friend and listen to him planning a future in which she should have had a big part and had none. . . The absurd idea that perhaps if she did so he might change his mind, discover that he couldn't bear to leave her behind after all, crossed her mind. 'All right,' she said, 'but I want to be back fairly early, I've a heavy list in the morning.'

The evening from her point of view had been an abject failure. Tom had enthused about his job until she could have thrown a plate at him; he seemed to have taken their broken engagement in his stride, over-shadowed as it was by an exciting future. Lying in bed, wide awake when she should have been recruiting her strength for the next day's work, Amelia vowed there would be no more little dinners with Tom.

It had been difficult to avoid him, but she had managed it, going out a good deal, visiting family who lived in London, shopping for the wedding outfit, rushing off home for her days off. She was able to wish him the best of luck when he came round to say goodbye, her voice nice and steady while her heart felt like lead. How wonderful it would be if one could say exactly what one wished on such occasions instead of uttering meaningless phrases. She cried herself to sleep that night and then got up early to do things to her red eyes and nose. The wedding was on the following day and she had her days off for it, staying with a great-aunt who lived rather grandly in Belgravia. At all costs, she must look her best.

By the time she went down to breakfast she was looking almost as pretty as usual and no one remarked upon her still pink nose and eyelids. Everyone knew by now that Tom had gone for good and that their engagement was over and although no one had said anything, they had been very kind. They laughed and joked about the wedding now, giving her little opportunity to think. And the day was a busy one, with Mr Thomley-Jones at his rattiest and a new student nurse to guide. She wasn't going to be any good, anyway, Amelia decided; she would have to go to the office and ask if she could be sent on to a ward while someone with a little more phlegm took her place. Not that Amelia blamed the girl; not everyone took to theatre, but this girl really shouldn't have closed her eyes when she handed the surgeon a kidney dish in which he intended to deposit various inner portions of the patient on the table, nor should she have screamed when Mr Thomley-Jones, getting impatient, threw a pair of forceps across the theatre. One needed strong nerves to work for him, and the poor girl hadn't got them. Amelia had a little chat with her before she went off duty and warned her staff nurse to be sure and keep her well away from theatre for the next day or two. 'I'll see the office when I get back,' said Amelia, 'and try and get her changed.'

The little problem kept her mind busy while she changed that evening; it was November now, cold and dark and wet. She put on her suit, topped it with the mink coat her father had given her for her birthday, perched a fur cap on her head, made sure that she had all she needed in her case, and left the hospital, trying not to remember the number of times she had taken those same passages on her way to spending an evening with Tom.

She drove herself to her aunt's house and found her father already there talking to her great-aunt, a rather forbidding lady who greeted her with: 'Well, my dear Amelia, so you've broken your engagement. I daresay it's for the best, but one must remember that you're no longer a young girl.'

Amelia cast around in her mind for a suitable answer and was grateful to her father for asking her loudly if she could do with a drink before dinner.

The meal was a stately affair. Her aunt had made no attempt to keep up with the younger generations and Amelia had taken care to bring a silk jersey dress with her, a discreet long-skirted, long-sleeved affair which blended very nicely with the austere furnishings of the vast dining room. And afterwards she went early to bed with the excuse that she had had a hard day and wanted to look her best for the following day's ceremony.

The wedding was to be at two o'clock and Amelia took her time getting ready for it. She had spent a good deal of money and time on her outfit—a café-au-lait wool crêpe dress and jacket and a large-brimmed melusine hat of exactly the same shade, trimmed with a taffeta ribbon. She looked quite beautiful in it and she made up her face with great care too and pinned on the sapphire and diamond brooch which had been her mother's. Her patent leather shoes matched her handbag exactly and her gloves were very soft suede. Even her great-aunt, resplendent in velvet and furs, remarked upon the charm of her appearance and her father, never one to notice clothes, pronounced that in his opinion Amelia would outshine the bride.

She had neither expected nor wanted to do that; all the same it was gratifying to see so many heads turn as they walked to their pew. Among every colour of the rainbow, Amelia's elegant clothes couldn't fail to be noted. She exchanged nods and smiles with various of her family sitting round her, settled her great-aunt beside her and composed her face into an expression of someone about to enjoy the ceremony. It was like turning the knife in the wound, she thought. She could have been the one walking up the aisle. She stopped thinking about it, shutting her mind ruthlessly to everything but the present, otherwise she might burst into tears.

The organ, which had been providing gentle background music for some time, suddenly became very loud; the bride had arrived. No expense had been spared; Barbara, decked out in white satin, yards of old family lace and her granny's pearls, came down the aisle, clinging to her father's arm— a thing she wasn't in the habit of doing, for they didn't much care for each other—and followed by what Amelia considered to be far too many bridesmaids. They were all ages and sizes and they were all wearing an insipid pink which did nothing for them, especially the one cousin in the family with flaming red hair. She and Amelia were good friends even though they didn't meet often; she winked as she swanned along behind the bride.

Amelia didn't pay too much attention to the service. She knew that if she did she would start thinking about Tom and she had vowed not to do that. Various members of the family and their friends were bound to ask her when she was going to get married and she had rehearsed a number of answers so that she wouldn't be taken by surprise. As she stood there, singing 'The voice that breathed o'er Eden' in an unselfconscious soprano, any casual observer might have been forgiven for thinking her to be one of the happiest people in the church.

It took a long time for the congregation to leave once the bride and her groom had driven away. Almost everyone there knew everyone else and there was a good deal of lingering while gossip was exchanged. Amelia and her father were among the last to get into their car which Badger, wearing a peaked cap for the occasion, was driving. The reception was being held in Barbara's home, a solid residence in a solid square, where the houses were still houses and not flats and the residents held little keys to the garden in the centre. The house was large and after her own home Amelia found it ugly, too full of furniture and as many modern gadgets as could be crowded in among it; she had disliked it as a little girl, she disliked it even more now. She gave her father a nudge as they went up the wide staircase and they paused for a moment to gaze unbelievingly at a modern painting which looked like the enthusiastic efforts of a very small child.

'Ghastly,' breathed Mr Crosbie. 'Let's get inside and find the champagne—I need it!'

But first there were the parents of the bride and groom and the happy couple to greet. Amelia offered her cheek and pecked the air in a polite greeting, said all the right things and turned to look round the big room, now packed to overflowing with guests. She knew a great many people, of course; she nodded and smiled to those near enough, waved to those who were too far away for the exchange of greetings and wandered a little further. She stopped so suddenly that one or two people nearby gave her a curious stare, but she didn't see that. What she saw was Gideon at the other end of the room, standing head and shoulders above everyone else, talking to a pretty red-haired girl. At least, he had been talking to her, presumably, now he was staring at Amelia over everyone else's head. She tried to smile, a meaningless social smile, but her mouth shook so that she turned her head away quickly.

'Now this is a delightful surprise,' said Gideon from somewhere close behind her. 'I had no idea that you knew the bride.'

'She's my cousin,' she gave him a fleeting glance and looked away again, 'we've known each other all our lives.' She added lightly, wishing very much to know: 'And you? I hardly expected. . .'

'Oh, I'm a friend of the groom's.' He tucked a hand under her elbow and began to work his way through the press of people around them.

'I don't really want. . .' began Amelia.

He took no notice, but when he reached a wall, he stood her up against it, took two glasses of champagne from a passing waiter and stationed himself in front of her so that she couldn't see anything or anyone, only his vast person, attired so correctly in morning coat and grey waistcoat.

'And how is Tom?' He asked the question idly, but his eyes were sharp under their lowered lids.

She took a gulp of champagne. 'He's fine.'

'Any plans to follow in your cousin's footsteps?'

'Not just yet. He's—he's got a super job, though.'

'Indeed? Where?'

She had been a fool to have told him that. Now she would have to tell fibs, for the very last thing she was going to do was to let him know that Tom had gone. She finished the champagne and said: 'I'd like some more, please,' which gave her a few seconds in which to think up something, only she didn't. She wondered instead what he would say if she told him that she had made a discovery; that it wasn't Tom at all whom she loved but he, standing there smiling at her. 'Across a crowded room,' she thought a trifle wildly. She felt peculiar again; she had felt like that when she had met Gideon for the first time and she knew now, with all the clarity of hindsight, that she had fallen in love with him then and had never allowed herself to acknowledge it.

She tossed off most of the champagne and Gideon said, half laughing: 'You'll be stoned if you drink any more.' He smiled at her lazily. 'You look delightful; very *grande dame*. I like the hat and your hair bundled up like that.'

'*Bundled?*' she began indignantly. 'It took hours and it's stuffed with pins. I really ought to circulate.'

'Presently. There's a song—I'm strongly reminded of it—''Some enchanted evening,'' although the only line appropriate to us is the one ''Across a crowded room''.'

'Oh, did you think of that? So did I.'

'Now that's interesting, Amelia. And why do you look so sad? You looked sad in church too, but perhaps you don't know that.'

She wanted desperately to put out her hand and clutch his arm and explain why she was sad, and not because of Tom, who had suddenly become quite unimportant, but because she loved him so much and he didn't care two straws for her.

'I'm very happy,' she said a shade too loudly. As the waiter went past she took another glass of champagne.

'Happy? Oh yes, and I'm sure you will be - because you will make your own happiness. You'll tend it with all the care of someone holding a last candle in the dark. You'll learn to make do with second best; a great many men and women do, you know. Just a few know what real happiness is— to love someone so much that nothing else matters any more, only the two of you and the life you share.' Gideon smiled faintly. 'We could have been like that, you and I. You know that deep in your heart, don't you, my darling? And do you know something else? If it would make you happy, I would give up all I have and live in a desert with you, or on top of a mountain. I'd pluck the moon from the sky and hang the stars round your beautiful neck. The world could be paradise.' He sighed. 'But most of us, as I said, make do with second best.'

Amelia drank in every word, her insides glowing with excitement. He loved her—he must, to talk to her like that. She had only to explain. . .

The next minute she knew that she never would. He laughed suddenly and the mockery in his laugh was so blatant that she winced. 'What nonsense one talks at weddings! Come and meet Fiona; we came together—we've known each other for a long time.'

Amelia felt numb. Presently she was going to feel simply frightful, but now shock and champagne had made everything dreamlike. She allowed herself to be led across the room to where the red-haired girl was talking to a small group of people, smiled and chatted and laughed gaily at the usual little social jokes, drank, very unwisely, some more champagne, and contrived not to look at Gideon at all. Presently she was able to excuse herself on the grounds of having a talk with friends whom she hadn't seen for some time, and drifted away, smiling vaguely at everyone as she went.

Barbara and her husband left soon afterwards and the guests began to leave too, slowly at first and then in a steady stream until there were only a dozen or so members of the family left. Amelia, chattering feverishly to an uncle she hadn't met in years, watched with despair as the pretty redhead made a graceful exit with Gideon at her heels. He had said his goodbyes, but not to her, only a casual wave of the hand as he reached the door.

Amelia managed to delay her own departure for another ten minutes, despite her father's impatience, and when at last they went out into the street where Badger was waiting with the car there was no sign of Gideon. It was very foolish of her to feel disappointed.

'I had a chat with Gideon,' remarked Mr Crosbie as they settled themselves in the car. 'Extraordinary meeting him again like that. You had a talk with him, of course?'

'Yes, just for a minute or two.' Amelia kept her voice casual with a great effort. 'It—it was strange seeing him there.' A sudden horrible thought made her exclaim: 'Father, you didn't say anything about Tom and me?'

'Certainly not, my dear. Didn't think he'd be interested, anyway. Very wrapped up in that pretty girl—old Boucher's youngest daughter, wasn't she?—got a funny name; F something. . .'

'Fiona— yes, he was. If you ever see him again, though I don't suppose you will, don't tell him anything, Father, please.'

'Just as you say, my dear.' He shot her a quick glance she didn't see. 'But it's highly unlikely that we shall, you know.'

'Yes, I know that. Father, do you suppose Aunt will mind if I go back to St Ansell's directly after dinner? I've a busy morning tomorrow. I can get a taxi, there's no need to get Badger out again.'

They dined in state again, while her aunt carried on a monologue about the wedding, not really wanting anyone to do more than agree with her from time to time, and Amelia was glad to escape presently. She bade her elders goodbye, got into the taxi fetched for her, and found herself half an hour later in her room at the home. It looked small and sparsely furnished after the spacious one at her aunt's house, but at least it was quiet and she could sit and think, but not for long, unfortunately. Her friends, coming off duty one by one, wandered in and out wanting to know about the wedding while they offered cups of tea or perched on her bed to talk. It was late by the time she was alone again, but she didn't go to sleep; she sat up in bed, trying to understand how she could have been

in love with Gideon and not known about
it and how, she wondered unhappily, was
she going to get through the rest of her life
without him, never seeing him or speaking
to him again? It didn't bear thinking about,
and much worse than that was knowing that
he didn't care a button for her.

'It's no good crying over spilt milk,'
she admonished herself out loud, and
promptly did.

CHAPTER SIX

CHRISTMAS was very near. Amelia went about the task of buying presents with a complete lack of enthusiasm. Instead of looking at handbags, ties and belts for all her numerous relations, she found herself in the Burlington Arcade, staring at men's cashmere sweaters, picturing Gideon in them. It really would not do, she told herself furiously, prowling round Harrods in search of something for Bonny, only to fetch up at a counter displaying ties. She had chosen several, all pure silk and very expensive, in her mind before she was able to stop herself.

She would be on duty for the whole of Christmas this year, keeping the theatre in a state of readiness with the aid of a skeleton staff, and she wasn't sorry about this. They were bound to be busy. The holiday periods were always worse when it came to emergencies and she would have no time to think about her own affairs. There were several parties and dances she would go to, of course, for the family was a large one and any number of them lived in London.

Amelia spent time in the choosing of some new outfits for these functions, and a great deal of money too. Barbara and her husband had invited her to an evening party on the day after Boxing Day, and she had found just the thing for it; a french navy chiffon over a satin slip, lavishly embroidered with sequins. She had been extravagant over her shoes too, for they were ridiculous satin ones which she would only wear with that particular dress, but she knew she would look eye-catching—although just whose eye she wanted to catch was something she didn't go too deeply into. At the very back of her head she cherished the forlorn hope that Gideon might be there, but common sense told her that he wouldn't. Christmas was a family time, he wouldn't go gadding about in another country—besides, she had made it her business to find out that the pretty redhead had gone to America. . .

She went home for her days off the week before Christmas and found her father, oblivious of the festive season, deep in his armchair, reading. But Bonny had everything in hand. She assured Amelia that there would be a tree as usual, and plenty of holly and mistletoe and an abundance of mince pies for the carol singers when they paid their annual visit. 'And a pity you can't be here, Miss Amelia, you oughtn't to be cooped up in that nasty theatre—it can't be healthy.'

She eyed Amelia's well-rounded figure, bursting with good health, with indulgent affection.

Amelia gave her a hug. 'I'm always covered up,' she assured her old friend. 'Besides, I'm not working all the time, you know, I'm going to quite a few parties.'

'Well, I'm glad to hear it. Will you be coming down at all over the holidays?'

'I'll try. The aunts will be here, of course?'

The aunts were her mother's two sisters, rather formidable elderly ladies who had loved her mother very deeply and now considered it to be their duty to keep an eye on her father. This meant regular visits, tolerated by Bonny and Badger and suffered by her father. Amelia liked them both, much more than the toffee-nosed aunts and cousins who lived in London. 'I'll really do my best to come down directly after Christmas,' she promised, and went along to stir up her father into taking some interest in the giving of presents.

She drove back to London the next day, hating to leave the peace and quiet of her home but glad that she was going to be fully occupied for the next week. And not only with theatre cases; off-duty times were taken up with helping the medical students get their costumes for the annual hospital concert. This was a traditional thing. Christmas wouldn't have been Christmas without it; invariably there was a sketch in which Matron largely figured, and a chorus line of stalwart rugger players rigged out in ballet costume. Amelia, handy with her needle, spent a good deal of time stitching and making wigs from crêpe paper, and even in theatre the surgeons would discuss the forthcoming entertainment with a kind of nostalgia because they were now too senior and too important to join in the fun themselves.

There were the wards to decorate, too. Amelia's friends all had wards of their own, and a good deal of time was spent in arguing the virtues of fancy head-dresses for the nurses or whether there ought to be potted meat sandwiches for the patients' tea as well as Christmas cake and chocolate biscuits. And through all this activity, the work had to go on as usual, and just as Amelia had anticipated, theatre was in constant use. Fractured skulls, smashed faces and some quite nasty stab wounds, the result of the victims and their friends toasting the festive season rather too liberally, followed each other with almost monotonous regularity, interlarded by acute obstructions, appendices, stones in kidneys, stones in gall bladders and rather more road accidents than usual, and these needing all the skill which could be offered them. Amelia went off duty late night after night and slept like a log, far too tired to think about anything except keeping the theatre running smoothly.

Which she did, showing an unflurried front

on Christmas morning when three road accident victims were sent up, one after the other. She ate her Christmas dinner, saved for her in the hot-plate and by then glued to it, so that it looked like the miniature dinners served to the occupants of dolls' houses, by herself before rushing back to lay up for another patient, a small girl who had somehow contrived to swallow an open safety pin which was now playing havoc with her small insides. It was tea-time before they had finished, and Amelia had a quick cup in her office and since there was nothing for the moment, left her student nurse in charge with instructions to get her at once should the need arise, made her way from ward to ward, to admire the decorations, drink whatever was offered her and then find her way to the main surgical ward where the concert would have its first airing.

She sat and giggled happily at the antics of the students for a little while and then went back to theatre again to take the nurse's place while she watched the rest of the show, and although there were no more cases, there was plenty for her to do and while she did it she thought with relief that in two days' time she would be out herself at Barbara's party; perhaps not exactly the entertainment she would have chosen, but it would be fun to dress up and not feel the need to dash to the phone each time it rang. There was a drinks party too, at an aunt's house, and the day before that dinner with her father's brother and his wife. She had more than enough to look forward to.

Boxing Day was even busier, partly because people went visiting relations and drove carelessly or fell in front of buses or tripped up on the pavements. She was so tired at the end of the day that she almost decided not to go to any parties at all, but retire to bed each evening with a book and a bag of apples. But she felt better in the morning and Staff Nurse was there to relieve her at lunch time, then she had a whole blissful afternoon in which to do nothing before dressing for Barbara's party. She not only did nothing; she fell sound asleep and woke just in time to take a quick shower, gulp down a cup of tea made by one of her friends and tear into the new dress.

All the same, when she was ready, she looked cool and composed and had the air of one who had spent hours on a leisurely toilette. She displayed her outfit to an admiring audience of friends, wrapped herself in the feather-light mohair wrap her father had given her for Christmas, and tripped downstairs mindful of the new slippers. She wasn't going to drive herself; the lodge porter called a taxi for her, told her that she looked a treat and sent her on her way.

Barbara and her husband had a flat just

behind Sloane Square. Amelia could hear the party as she got out and paid the driver and the noise got worse as she soared up to the fourth floor in the lift. The block was an expensive one, floored by lush carpets and with a lot of wrought iron about. The flat door wasn't open, but Amelia decided quite rightly that no one was going to hear her ring anyway, so she opened it and walked in.

Probably she was the last to arrive. She added her wrap to the pile of mink and red fox on the huge sofa which took up the whole of one wall in the hall, and went unhurriedly into the drawing room.

It was packed, and judging by the noise and laughter, a wild success. Amelia edged her way slowly towards Barbara, standing at the other end of the room, wearing a hideous red dress which made her look fat. As she went she smiled and nodded and mouthed greetings to such of those whom she knew and wondered where the food was. She had slept through tea, and the one cup she had had was gurgling around inside her in a disconcerting way. She reached her cousin at last and received a peck on her cheek which she returned politely, murmuring appreciation of the party, remarking on Barbara's splendid appearance and hoping she was enjoying life.

'Of course I am,' Barbara said with a small snigger. 'You should have got married,

Amelia, even if it wasn't exactly a brilliant match. How do you like being a bachelor girl again?'

'I've never been anything else, and I'd rather make up my mind as to my future before I got married. . .it must be difficult once you're tied down, even in these days.' Amelia smiled into Barbara's cross face and floated away in her sparkling dress, to be instantly surrounded by a number of men acquaintances. She couldn't resist a small smile at her cousin as she accepted a glass from one of them. She eyed the glass doubtfully: someone had said it was a cup, and knowing Barbara she was pretty sure that it had been prepared with an eye to economy. She took a cautious sip and knew she was right; it tasted like watered-down raspberry jam with bits of apple and cucumber in it. Really, Barbara should know better! She exchanged party chat for a few minutes and then declared firmly that she had any number of uncles and aunts to speak to, and took herself off, discarding the more persistent of her followers with a disarming charm.

She made for her favourite aunt, her father's elder sister, a mild-looking lady whose good looks bore witness to the fact that in her youth she must have been as pretty as her niece. Her 'Hullo, darling', was uttered with real pleasure. 'How gorgeous you look! What a filthy drink this is. Barbara could surely afford champagne. . . Your father told me you were working over Christmas. How's life?' Her kind eyes searched Amelia's face. 'I was sorry to hear about you and Tom he wasn't the right man for you, darling, but that's such a stupid thing to say, isn't it?' Her eyes focused over Amelia's shoulder. 'Ah, there's that nice man I met. . .' She lifted a hand and beckoned and Amelia turned to see who it was. Gideon.

She went a little pale and then as he reached them, blushed charmingly. He greeted them both pleasantly, said all the right things to her aunt and then turned to her. 'What a pleasant surprise. I imagined you to be at your home with Tom. . .were you not free for the holiday?'

Amelia was having an absurd difficulty in speaking, her breath had left her and she couldn't think of anything to say—an omission filled by Barbara who had strolled over to join them. 'Amelia with Tom?' she laughed gaily. 'You must be joking, Gideon! You must know—everyone does—he's in Australia and they decided not to get married after all. Fancy not knowing; it's been a nine days' wonder around the family.'

Gideon's face remained politely interested, no more. 'But I'm not family, Barbara.' He glanced at Amelia. 'I'm sorry to hear it. When did this happen?'

Amelia didn't get a chance to answer him,

although she wasn't sure if she was going to. He had no right to question her. . .

Barbara told him, smiling at her as she did so, but Amelia didn't see that. She watched Gideon and knew at once that he remembered when they had met and she hadn't said a word about it. The bland expression hadn't altered, but his eyes were gleaming under their heavy lids. She wondered just for a moment if he were laughing.

'I really must go and talk to Uncle George,' she smiled at all three of them, her chin well up. She put her glass down on a nearby table. 'That's a most unusual cup, Barbara,' she murmured, 'it's quite gone to my head.'

Uncle George was a haven; a large stout old man whose bulk shielded her nicely from the rest of the room. She stood exchanging gentle conversation with him and wondered how soon she could get away. The evening was a failure, the dress had been a wicked waste of money, she might just as well have worn a sack. . .

Uncle George paused in his gentle droning. 'My dear fellow, how delightful to see you again! You know my niece Amelia, of course. Lord, yes, foolish of me, you were on holiday together. Take her away, will you, and find her some food; she tells me she's quite famished.'

Gideon's large hand propelled her gently through the crowd. 'I like the dress,' he observed from somewhere above her head. 'I have always considered that big girls look splendid in evening outfits.'

Amelia managed to come to a halt. 'Really,' she declared loftily, 'whatever will you say next? And I'm not a big girl!'

He still had a hand under her elbow although he was making no effort to move. 'You are, you know. Of course I could describe you in somewhat different terms, but I doubt if you would wish me to.'

'Certainly not!' She took a deep breath. Really, she wasn't going to be able to stay with him a minute longer. She might say something silly like how very glad she was to see him again and had he missed her. Of course he hadn't. She said rather desperately: 'Oh, there's an aunt I haven't seen for years. . .'

He began edging her forward again. 'In that case, she probably won't recognise you. Your Uncle George says you are to have something to eat. Have you been on a diet?'

'Certainly not!'

'Pining for Tom?' he asked softly.

She didn't answer him. Extraordinary, she thought, how one can love someone who could be so annoying and so persistent. She stuck her beautiful nose into the air. 'That's my business.'

'Indeed, yes. I'm merely inquisitive, but as my grandmother always said: ''There's many more fish in the sea''.'

'I'm not interested in your grandmother.'

'A pity; she would have liked you.'

They had reached the dining room where a long table was laid out with an assortment of food on silver salvers. They roamed its length and finally Amelia said: 'I think I'll stay famished.'

And indeed the feast set out before them wasn't particularly appetising. Carrot sticks hardly filled anyone, not unless they were dieting fiercely. The cheese straws bent in a rubbery fashion when Amelia picked one up and the canapés were no more than tiny appetisers.

'Never mind,' said Gideon. 'We'll get called away urgently and have dinner somewhere.' He said it in such a casual way that she had agreed before she had time for second thoughts and when she did have them she turned a metaphorical back on them.

'Are you a good liar?' asked Gideon as they started fighting their way back to the drawing room.

'When absolutely necessary, yes.'

She managed very well. With just the right amount of urgency and regret she made it clear to Barbara that there had been a message for her to go back to the hospital— there was a case and one theatre was already being used.

Barbara didn't believe her, of course, but

she uttered little cries of sympathy, urged Amelia to come again whenever she had a free moment and proffered her cheek once more.

'I'll run Amelia back; it won't take more than a few minutes.' Gideon somehow gave the impression that he would be back in no time at all and Barbara believed him. Only Aunt Delia, her pretty elderly face quite without expression, gave him a piercing glance as she kissed her niece.

There was a dark blue Rolls parked at the kerb as they left the building and Gideon unlocked its doors and helped her in.

'Yours?' asked Amelia as he got in beside her.

'Yes. How about Le Gavroche?'

'We'll never get in.'

'Yes, we will.' He didn't enlarge upon his hopeful remark and the drive was so short that there was hardly time to find out why. But they were shown to a table immediately and as they sat down Amelia asked: 'How did you do it?'

'I was able to help one of the owners a year or so ago, when he was taken ill.'

She waited for more, but it seemed that was all she was to know. She said rather crossly: 'What I like about you is the generous way you hand out information.'

He looked unperturbed. 'As long as there's something you like about me, Amelia.' He added: 'And if I might say so, you haven't been all that forthcoming yourself. Why didn't you tell me about Tom?'

'Why should I? I didn't think you'd be interested. Do you mind if we don't talk about it?'

'No, I don't mind in the least. To quote your own words: Why should I?' His smile was faintly mocking. 'Now let's settle the most important question of what we are going to eat. And what would you like to drink? I must admit that the drinks at your cousin's party tasted very peculiar; soda water, cider probably with a dash of gin and a bottle of plonk with the merest trace of red ink to give it colour.'

Amelia giggled. 'I thought it was watered-down raspberry jam. I only had a sip—it might have played havoc with my insides. It was my first Christmas party too.'

Gideon smiled, kindly now, for she looked like a disappointed child dressed for a party and then told that she wouldn't be going. 'You didn't get home?'

She shook her head, suddenly quite at ease with him. Loving him had nothing to do with it, she discovered; he was just very nice to be with. 'No, it was my turn to be on duty this year, I'll go home for my days off.'

He looked up from the menu. 'When is that?'

'Oh, two days' time. There's a dinner

tomorrow and a drinks party the evening after, both family, and I'd like to go, though they won't be very exciting—not that Barbara's was that.'

'I found it very exciting.' His voice was blandly casual, and Amelia wondered miserably which of the girls there had taken his fancy.

But it was hard to be miserable with a champagne cocktail inside her and a delicious meal, beautifully served with more champagne to wash it down. She spooned the last mouthful of the light-as-air sorbet and sat back with a contented sigh. 'That was one of the nicest meals I've ever eaten,' she assured Gideon, 'and thank you very much for asking me out.'

'A pleasure; Barbara's party snacks were hardly sufficient to satisfy one, and eating alone is a lonely business.'

She remained silent while the waiter served their coffee. 'Then I'm even more in your debt than I imagined. There were a dozen girls who would have entertained you far better than I.'

His imperturbable: 'Oh, I daresay,' made her choke with temper. 'But after all, we share a kind of friendship, do we not? Do you ever think about Norway?'

She said coldly: 'Oh, frequently—it was a delightful holiday. I think Father and I will go again next year.'

'Yes, he was telling me about it. . .'

'When was that? While we were on holiday?'

'No, no—I went down to see him a week ago. I had a rod he was interested in. I am going again, just for the night—as a matter of fact on the same day as you plan to go. Perhaps I may give you a lift.'

Her heart fluttered and bumped around under the lovely dress, but she answered him with composure. 'That's nice of you, but I usually drive down, then I can get back.'

'I'll drive you back too.'

'But you said one night.'

'Don't split hairs, Amelia. Another day won't upset my practice too much—I've a partner, you know. A change will do you good, you mustn't be allowed to pine for Tom. I daresay he'll come back for you and sweep you off to wherever it is he is and you'll be happy ever after. Never give up hope—I don't.'

She almost wailed at him: 'But you don't have to!'

His smile was gently mocking. 'But you don't know anything about me, do you, Amelia? You don't know when I'm serious and when I'm joking, do you? For all you know I may be hiding a broken heart. After all, I'm thirty-six, by rights I should be married with a flourishing family.'

Amelia looked at him with sudden apprehension. 'And are you?' she asked anxiously. 'Hiding a broken heart, I mean.'

Gideon handed her his cup for more coffee. 'Not quite broken, but badly bruised.'

She poured the coffee and refilled her own cup. 'I'm so sorry,' she said gently, and then wished she hadn't when he said cheerfully, 'Oh, she'll be back.'

So it was the redhaired girl, old Boucher's daughter. 'She's only gone for a couple of weeks, Barbara told me.'

His voice was bland although his eyes were gleaming. 'Surely we know each other well enough to use names?' he asked.

'Of course—sorry. It's Fiona, isn't it? She's the daughter of an old friend of Father's. I don't see her very often, only if we happen to be at the same party.'

'And do you have time to go to parties, Amelia?'

She shook her head, glad that the conversation was getting back to general topics again. 'No, not often. Christmas, of course, and weddings and christenings, and so on.'

'And New Year?'

'Oh, I've got an extra day for that because I worked over Christmas; I'm looking forward to it.'

'Well, it seems a pity to waste the pretty dress on a mere dinner—shall we go and dance somewhere?'

'Oh, yes, please. But if you don't mind,

not for too long, I'm on duty in the morning and there's one of Mr Thomley-Jones' lists.'

'I promise to get you back at a reasonable hour.' He smiled at her, and list or no list, Amelia wouldn't have minded if he had suggested that they danced until morning.

She crawled into bed at two o'clock, her tired head full of the delights of the evening. They had danced endlessly, had supper about midnight and danced again. She remembered that once or twice she had said without conviction that she really would have to go back to the hospital, but somehow neither of them took any notice. It was while they were dreamily waltzing on the crowded floor that Gideon asked: 'What is the first case in the morning?'

'A cholystectomy with complications.'

'In that case I'll take you back—a few hours' sleep will get you into shape for Mr Thomley-Jones' uncertain temper.'

And he hadn't wasted time. She had been whisked back and deposited at the door of the nurses' home, and when she had thanked him he had spoilt it all by remarking casually that he had enjoyed their evening too and how lucky that he had come upon her, otherwise he might have been condemned to a solitary evening. Amelia hadn't been able to think of a crushing answer to that, she had been too tired. 'But I shan't go home with him,' she promised herself in a pettish voice as she closed her eyes.

Contrary to her gloomy forebodings, when she got up the next morning, the list went without a hitch, although she had no time at all to sort out her own muddled thoughts. The previous evening had been enjoyable and at the same time most unsatisfactory. And she had no time when she went off duty to give her feelings the attention she would wish; it wasn't a big dinner party, but she knew everyone there. The evening passed pleasantly, although she had to admit to herself afterwards that compared with the previous one, it had been dull. 'And that's what you get for falling in love with someone like Gideon,' she admonished herself as she prepared for bed.

She wore one of her new dresses to the drinks party. Aunt Delia was giving it and although she looked such a mild unassuming person she had strong ideas about how people should dress for parties. So Amelia put on a pleated crêpe-de-chine dress in a becoming shade of claret, wound her hair into a chignon into which she stuck two jewelled combs, made up her face with extra care, sprayed herself with *l'Air du Temps* and teetered downstairs on a pair of ridiculous, high-heeled satin sandals which had cost her the earth. It was well worth it, though, for Aunt Delia, in grey lace and diamonds, gave the outfit her instant approval. 'You have a splendid dress sense, my dear,' she exclaimed, 'such a pretty girl too.' She looked pleased with herself and Amelia wondered idly what she had been up to, and then forgot it as she joined the other guests.

Unlike Barbara, Aunt Delia, when she gave a party, provided excellent drink and super food. She disliked what she termed modern drinks; granted, the men were allowed whisky, otherwise there was sherry, gin and tonic and a variety of soft drinks. But the sherry was of the finest and so was the whisky, and the dishes of tiny sausage rolls, smoked salmon and tiny biscuits carefully topped with caviare were invariably emptied and the bowls of walnuts and cream cheese, stuffed dates and olives were emptied as fast as they were filled. Amelia was standing, her hand hovering over some appetising prunes stuffed with ginger, when Gideon's quiet voice sent her spinning round.

'Your aunt's parties are definitely not to be missed.'

'How did you get here?' Amelia's breath was a little short.

'I was invited.'

'But you don't know anyone. . .'

'Your aunt was so kind as to ask me to come along—we met at Barbara's.'

'Oh, yes, of course—how stupid of me.'

She stood staring at him, trying to think of

something offhand to say, and it was a relief when Aunt Delia joined them.

'That's right, my dears, do try those prunes – my cook thought them up, but I'm not sure if people will take to them.' She beamed at them. 'So nice that you both know each other.'

'Why should it be nice?' demanded Amelia when her aunt had gone, and wished instantly that she hadn't said it.

'I expect she thought that I might have been lonely,' Gideon said silkily.

'Bunkum!' She ate a prune.

His eyes widened with laughter. 'If you say so. Can I get you another drink?'

'No, thanks, I've had two sherries already.'

'Very abstemious, and unnecessary too, as you won't be driving.'

'I'm not going this evening.' Amelia ate another prune and thought how very nice Gideon looked in his black tie.

'Well, it struck me that it might be a good idea to drive down after this we can dine on the way and be at your home soon after eleven, probably sooner.'

'I'm driving myself down tomorrow.'

'Oh, dear your father's expecting you this evening; he took it for granted that you would come with me.' Gideon ate a prune thoughtfully. 'Afraid of my driving, Amelia?'

'Of course not. You're an excellent driver

and you know it, you've no need to fish for compliments.' She looked around her, anxious to end the conversation. 'I'm tired of prunes and there's an old friend I haven't spoken to yet.'

'I'm not sure if that's quite polite, but I gather you wish to be rid of me.' He smiled with charm to melt her heart and stood aside. As she went past him he observed pleasantly: 'What a very pretty dress —slimming, too.'

She swirled round to face him. 'You're the most objectionable man I've ever met!' and then stopped because he was laughing gently.

'I didn't say that you needed slimming, Amelia, I merely pointed out. . .'

'All right, I know.' She gave him a glacial nod. 'Goodbye, Gideon.'

She didn't speak to him for the rest of the party, although she was very aware of him moving from group to group, quite at home, too. As the guests began to leave she slid across the room to her aunt.

'Darling, I'm going to slip away, so don't call attention to me, will you? I don't want. . . It was a lovely party, and thank you very much.' She kissed her aunt, who wished her goodnight placidly, waited until she had gone and then hurried to where Gideon was standing watching.

Amelia, her pretty face buried in the angora wrap, tore out of the house, not waiting for Crawford, her aunt's butler, to make

his stately way into the street and call a cab.
She would find one easily enough, she
assured him, and nipped through the door he
opened for her.

The Rolls was at the kerb with Gideon
leaning against it. She had no time to say
more than: 'I will not. . .' before he had
opened the door, scooped her up and popped
her into the seat before slamming the
door again.

She sat staring in front of her while he got
in beside her. 'The M4 as far as Swindon
and then up to Cirencester, don't you agree?
Mansell Abbots can be reached easily from
there. We could eat at the White Hart in
Sonning.'

'Look,' she said in what she hoped was
a firm voice, 'you must be mad   I haven't
anything with me, I can't go home like this.'

'Why not? You look charming and I'm
sure you've got some clothes at home.'

Which was true – she had. 'I'm very tired,'
she muttered untruthfully, and was countered
by his soothing: 'Go to sleep, then, I'll wake
you at Sonning.'

Of course she didn't sleep. It was wonderful to be sitting beside him even though he
didn't utter a word, not until he slowed and
stopped at the White Hart. It didn't strike
Amelia until afterwards that there was a table
reserved for them; by now she was famished
and over her sherry discussed with enthusi-

asm what they would eat. They settled for bisque de homard and while she decided on a tournedos Rossini, Gideon settled for boeuf Stroganoff and the cheese board while Amelia finished off with ruche glacée. They drank their claret sparingly because they still had some way to go; all the same Amelia was in a pleasantly hazy state when they got back into the car.

The Rolls made short work of the run to Swindon. The motorway was almost empty and Gideon kept his foot down until they reached the town and swung off on to the Cirencester road, picking up speed again until he turned off once more, this time into a country road leading eventually to Mansell Abbots.

And all this time he had said very little, so that as they neared their journey's end she had asked a little peevishly: 'Don't you like to talk while you're driving?'

'But my dear girl, you told me you were tired.' He sounded like an indulgent uncle wheedling a pampered small niece.

'Well, I'm not any more.'

'Good, we're almost there. Aren't you glad you came? Driving at night is so much more relaxing; we've not passed a car for miles—just us and the dark. How very romantic!'

She agreed silently; it was only a pity that while she really did find it romantic he was only joking. A flippant reply would be nice, only she couldn't think of one.

'You don't agree?' he persisted, and when she stayed silent slowed the car and pulled into the side of the narrow road. Amelia turned her head to ask him why he had done that, but she didn't get as far as that; he kissed her very expertly and within seconds had sent the car shooting ahead again.

'Did that help?' he asked. 'It should, you know. I expect your ego is at an all-time low now that Tom has gone away.' He sounded pleasantly friendly. 'You need one or two— er—romantic interludes to get you back on to an even keel.'

She muttered something, thinking that it was bad enough loving him but far far worse to be the object of his pity. And at the same time she was simply livid with him. She sat, trying to sort out her various feelings, deeply thankful that home was just round the next bend. She would go to bed at once, she decided, and have a sick headache and stay in her room until he went away again. She never, she told herself savagely, wanted to set eyes on the wretch again.

CHAPTER SEVEN

AMELIA didn't find it quite as easy to carry out her plans as she had intended. For one thing her father was waiting for them and so were her two aunts, and after a good deal of kissing and hand-shaking, both she and Gideon were taken into the sitting room where a tray of sandwiches, little sausage rolls and tiny mince pies was arranged on one of the sofa tables, and Badger, after a discreet word of welcome, trotted in with coffee while Mr Crosbie offered drinks. Clearly it was to be a festive hour or so, and Amelia hadn't the heart to go straight to her room. Her father and aunts were so patently glad to see her and, it seemed to her sensitive ears, just as glad to welcome Gideon. So she sat down between her aunts and obligingly ate the food they pressed upon her and drank several cups of coffee while she told them about the parties she had been to and passed on all the messages she had been charged with. She didn't mention the hospital, as both of them disapproved of her working there, especially in the operating theatre, and they chatted on about their pleasant Christmas, ignoring the fact that Amelia hadn't had one.

And presently when they considered that she had eaten enough, they turned their attention to Gideon, who had been sitting opposite Mr Crosbie by the log fire, discussing the prospects for fishing in the next year, which meant, of course, that Amelia was drawn into a general conversation which lasted for another hour or more. Despite the brandy her father had given her she began to droop a little and the aunts urged her to go to her bed. She obeyed thankfully, kissed them goodnight, kissed her father too and paused to wish Gideon, who had gone to open the door for her, goodnight as well. The room was a large one and the three elderly people by the fire were talking together.

'Don't I get a kiss too?' he asked silkily, and then: 'No, perhaps not—it would be rather an anticlimax, wouldn't it?' He smiled down at her. 'Sleep well—you really are tired, aren't you?' His voice was suddenly so gentle that she felt the tears prick her eyelids and without saying anything turned and almost ran across the hall and up the staircase.

She stayed awake just long enough to remind herself that she was going to have a sick headache all the next day.

She was awakened by the steady patter of pebbles on the window. It was barely light, but a lovely morning with a pearly sky and no wind. There had been a frost and the air bit her as she flung open the window.

'Come on down,' begged Gideon, standing huge in a sheepskin jacket below her. 'A brisk walk will do you good.' He grinned suddenly. 'Only put some clothes on first.'

Amelia withdrew smartly, remembering just in time to say that she had a headache.

'All the more reason to come into the fresh air. Bonny told me to tell you that there's a cup of tea for you in the kitchen.' He stared up at her. 'Shall I come up and fetch you?'

'Certainly not. I'll be down in five minutes.' She hadn't meant to say that, she had had no intention of going out with him. She pulled on an old tweed skirt and a sweater and tied back her hair. Then she found a pair of boots and a rather tattered windcheater, snatched up a pair of gloves and went down to the kitchen, where she found Bonny and Gideon sitting at the table with the tea-pot between them.

'I really don't feel like going out,' said Amelia haughtily, and took the tea Bonny had poured for her.

'Now none of that nonsense, Miss Amelia,' admonished Bonny, 'the fresh air will do you a world of good after that nasty poisonous theatre of yours. Unhealthy, I call it, a nice girl like you poking about in people's insides.'

Amelia took a biscuit from the tin beside the tea-pot. 'Bonny dear, it's the surgeon who pokes. I only hand the things.'

'Well, it isn't nice. What do you think, Doctor?'

'Not nice at all,' agreed Gideon blandly. 'A woman's place is in the home, looking after her husband and children.'

'Don't be so old-fashioned,' snapped Amelia.

His voice was very mild. 'Well, you know, I don't think that families and home-making and being married will ever be out of fashion. You've changed your opinions pretty smartly, Amelia. I had the impression that being a wife was something you were looking forward to——before Tom and you parted, of course.'

She stared at him wordlessly. Tom didn't mean anything to her any more, but he wasn't to know that; he was being cruel. She got up from the table and plonked her mug down hard. 'That was a nice cup of tea,' she remarked icily. 'Enjoy your walk.'

She stalked from the room and made for the staircase, but not quite quickly enough. Gideon caught up with her as she had her foot on the bottom step and gripped her arm firmly. 'You're going the wrong way,' he observed genially.

She couldn't do much about it; he was twice her size and twice as heavy too. She gave in and walked through the front door beside him, looking haughtily in front of her. Unfortunately, Gideon seemed unaware of her ill humour. He talked with disarming friendliness about everything under the sun, not seeming to notice her brief yeses and noes. But then something happened to make her forget her peevishness. They were walking along a narrow, high-hedged lane, the dead bracken and leafless briars silvered with frost, the grass beneath stiff and spiky. It was a movement among these spikes followed by a small pitiful cry which stopped Amelia in her tracks. She put out an urgent hand and caught Gideon's sleeve. 'There's something. . .a snare. . .'

He was already on his knees, gently freeing the rabbit caught by a hind leg in a wire snare. It was trembling with terror and even when it was free, lay motionless in his hands while he examined it.

'No bones broken,' he pronounced. 'A bruised leg, but it should heal.' He put the little creature in Amelia's arms. 'Hold it close for a few moments, it needs to warm up and recover from the shock.' He glanced at her face. 'And don't look like that, my dear.' He bent and kissed her gently on a cheek, a comforting kiss. 'There's one little beast that will live to see another day.'

Amelia held the furry little body close. 'Yes, I know, I'm silly and I ought to be used to this sort of thing by now, but I never shall be.' She looked up at Gideon. 'Will it be all right if I let it go now?'

'Let's see.' She set the rabbit down and it stayed motionless for a long moment and then whisked itself into the hedge.

'I had pet rabbits when I was a small boy,' observed Gideon, taking her arm in an abstracted manner. 'They lived in one of the barns near the house. I had dormice too and a tame crow as well as the kitchen cat and her kittens. Heaven knows how I ever found time to go to school! Now I have to be content with a dog and cats.' He paused to lean over a hedge, and since he was still holding her arm, Amelia perforce paused too. 'I hope my children will have the fun I did.'

She said in a startled voice: 'Oh, are you going to get married?'

'The idea had crossed my mind. How far does your father's property extend?'

Such a pointed change in the conversation couldn't be ignored. 'That line of trees at the other side of this field—that's one boundary and the land's his as far as the crossroads we're coming to. The village is part of the estate, but at the back of the house there's only the garden as far as the river. It's small compared to your home.'

They started back again, and now Amelia had forgotten about the sick headache. A day with Gideon would be pleasant; he was a restful companion when he wanted to be and amusing too. Perhaps after breakfast they could walk to the village and she could show him the ruined monastery and the row of cottages which were so picturesque that people came from miles around just to look at them. She ate a good breakfast in anticipation of the morning ahead of her, and then had her hopes dashed by her father's cheerful statement that he was taking Gideon into Cirencester to meet a friend of his, an authority on fly fishing. They would, he told her, have a most enjoyable morning and she would see them for lunch. 'There must be a great deal you want to do, my dear,' finished her parent vaguely.

She agreed very quickly and didn't look at Gideon. And when they had gone she mooned around, getting in Bonny's way until Badger coaxed her into the sitting room with a tray of coffee. Drinking it, she had ample opportunity to reflect that Gideon had shown no sign of disappointment at being deprived of her society; of course he imagined that she was still pining for Tom.

The men came back rather late and lunch was largely taken up with the fascinations of fly fishing, and although both of them were meticulous in including her in their conversation, Amelia had the strong feeling that she wasn't really necessary to their pleasure. They had their coffee at the table and she excused herself almost at once. She had promised to go to the vicarage to see Angela, the daughter of the house there, and would probably stay to tea. She was half way to the door when her father remembered that he had asked a few friends in for drinks that evening. 'A dozen or so, my dear, there's not much amusement for Gideon here and I thought a few new faces. . .'

She expressed delight at the idea and seethed inwardly. It would mean that dinner would be late for a start and her parent had a habit of asking people to take pot luck. Her two aunts had been out visiting and weren't expected back until the late afternoon, which meant that probably there would be bridge that evening; she could think of at least three old friends of her father who would be delighted to stay on for a meal and a game. And as if that weren't enough, Mr Crosbie went on: 'The Thursbys are coming over this evening and they'll bring Letty with them. We'll have one or two people in to lunch tomorrow, you'd better ask Angela, that'll make us eight. He chuckled richly: 'Gideon can take his pick—you're both pretty girls.'

The kind of remark a father would make, thought Amelia, flouncing upstairs to fetch her coat and scarf. She presumably had a squint and a face to go with it! She went out of the side door, pulling on her gloves as she went briskly through the yard and out of the back gate. It was a long way round to the village, but since Angela had no idea that she was spending the afternoon with her, she couldn't get there too early. In fact, she called in on one or two of the more elderly inhabitants of the little community. Most of them had at some time worked for her father and she had known them all since she was a child. It was almost three o'clock by the time she turned in at the vicarage gates.

Angela was a little younger than she was, a small, slim creature with a sweet nature and easily bullied. Amelia had fought her battles for her as a child and they were firm friends. She saw Amelia from a window and came to meet her. 'I was going to ring you this morning, but I thought you'd be taken up with that Dutch doctor the whole village is talking about. I saw him this morning as your father and he drove past; he's pretty super. Is he keen on you, Amelia?'

Amelia was taking off her outdoor things and adding them to the comfortable pile of miscellaneous garments strewn on the wide bench in the hall.

'No,' she made her voice bright and casual, 'he's come to see Father—they share a love of fishing, you know. He's very pleasant and all that—gave me a lift down and I expect he'll drive me back, but he's only being civil.'

'But you stayed with him on your way back from Norway—your father was telling Father.'

They had wandered into the large, shabby

living room. 'Only because Father wanted to go,' explained Amelia.

Angela looked disappointed. 'Oh, I've been thinking how nice for you if. . .I mean, now that Tom's gone. . .'

Amelia conjured up a smile. 'Nothing like that, Angela—he doesn't even like me particularly.' For good measure she added, 'We don't hit it off.'

They had sat down on the hearthrug already crowded by two elderly dogs and a nondescript cat. 'You're coming up for drinks this evening, aren't you? Good—and Father says will you come to lunch tomorrow—no one much, the aunts and us and three of Father's friends and you.'

'I'd love to, though I can never think of anything to say. Will Letty be there this evening? I can't think of anything to say to her either.'

'Who can? Her head's empty, I don't suppose she thinks of anything other than make-up and the latest hair-styles.' Amelia sounded waspish and didn't care. Letty had always annoyed her and now she was to be let loose on Gideon who would probably succumb to her tinkling laugh and exquisitely turned out person. If he was going to fall for anyone, she would rather it were Angela. No, that wasn't true, she would rather it were herself.

But there was little hope of that; his indifference was obvious even though he masked it with good manners. Amelia began to toy with the idea of a sick headache again, or even an urgent call from the hospital that she was wanted back immediately. . .

'You've not been the same since Tom went,' declared Angela. 'Do you feel very awful about it, Amelia?'

Amelia hesitated. She liked Angie very much, she was a dear girl and a kind one too, but she answered questions far too readily. . .there was always the chance that Gideon would get her into a corner and ever so casually winkle out anything he had a mind to know. 'Well, it was a terrific surprise, it took a bit of getting over. Thank heaven for work!'

Angela gave her a sympathetic glance. 'Poor old you! Have you heard from him?'

'No, it wouldn't be a good idea, would it? What are you going to wear this evening? I've got a quite nice dress I wore to Aunt Delia's party in London, but I'm wondering if it might not be a bit too grand—I'll keep it, I think, and wear that old pink thing I had last year. I left it at home and I haven't worn it in ages.'

'You always look lovely whatever you wear,' declared Angela without envy. 'Mother gave me a dress for Christmas— ever such a plain bodice and a pleated skirt— it's blue.'

'It sounds just the thing. What have you been doing with yourself—Father hinted that you'd captured Reggie Wray's eye. Have you?'

Angela blushed. 'Well, I don't know—we get on awfully well, but I'm sure I won't stand a chance if Letty comes swanning along.'

'Leave Letty to me,' said Amelia. 'Let's roast some chestnuts—I'm hungry!'

The old pink thing didn't look so bad when she had it on. It was no longer the height of fashion, of course, but it was pretty in an understated way and the colour suited her. She did her hair in an elaborate chignon and stuck a velvet bow in it and found a pair of bronze sandals she hadn't worn for ages. There would be so many people there that what one wore below the waist wouldn't be seen anyway. She went downstairs as soon as she was ready to see if Bonny wanted a hand, but the housekeeper assured her that everything was just as it should be, adding a rider to the effect that if Miss Amelia was going to sample everything there wouldn't be enough for anyone else. Amelia gave her a hug, told Badger that he looked splendid in his new jacket and made her way to the drawing room.

Her father was already there and so was Gideon, looking elegant in his dark suit and handsome too. It would be a tiresome evening, she decided, having to watch Letty at work charming him, as undoubtedly she would.

Amelia said hullo, thanked her father prettily when he complimented her upon her appearance and then busied herself making conversation with her two aunts who had just joined them. They were all having a drink when the first guests arrived and she had had no chance to say a word to Gideon. Nor did she for the greater part of the next two hours, only when Letty and her parents arrived. She happened to be standing with Angela and Gideon as they entered the room and he, glancing over their heads, said softly: 'Now, there is a very pretty girl.' He added, half laughing, 'Present company excepted, of course.'

Letty looked exquisite, the old pink thing became just that when compared with her slinky black crêpe and sequins. Amelia ground her splendid teeth, smiled delightfully and hurried him over to be introduced. As she rejoined Angela she said crossly: 'Well, that's the last we'll see of him until she goes. I only hope Father doesn't take it into his head to ask them to stay on for dinner.'

She circulated conscientiously after that and was relieved to see Letty and her parents make their way to the door as the other guests began to say goodbye. Letty broke away for a moment and came dancing towards her.

'Amelia, what a lovely party! I've had a super time. That lovely man—where did you find him? Not that you want him, do you, darling? I daresay you're still brokenhearted over Tom going off like that and leaving you.' Her eyes widened suddenly and she looked over Amelia's shoulder. 'Oh, there you are, Gideon—I was just telling Amelia that it doesn't matter what old rag she wears, she always looks gorgeous.'

Amelia choked on a torrent of rude words. 'That's a nice compliment, Letty,' she declared sweetly, 'I must remember to wear my old rags more often.' She smiled widely. 'Your mother's beckoning—you mustn't keep her waiting.'

Letty gave a little laugh and then changed it into an enchanting gurgle for Gideon's benefit. 'I suppose you wouldn't like to have dinner with us?' she suggested, fluttering her eyelashes at him.

Perhaps eyelashes didn't interest him, thought Amelia, watching, for he looked completely disinterested. 'Charming of you,' he said formally, 'but I'm dining here.'

Letty lifted a lovely shoulder. 'Oh, well, another time.' She shook hands lingeringly, nodded at Amelia and swam back across the room. When she had gone Amelia turned away. 'You'll excuse me for a moment, won't you?' she asked Gideon. 'There's something I must ask Bonny. . .'

She need not have bothered. He put out a large hand and anchored her gently beside him. 'I like your friend Angela,' he told her. 'There aren't enough girls like her around, but I must beg of you not to leave me with Letty for more than a couple of minutes if ever we should encounter each other again.' He looked down at her, smiling slowly. 'That was a mean trick, Amelia.'

'I don't know what you mean.' She flicked some imaginary crumbs off her dress and didn't look at him.

'Oh, yes, you do. Leaving me at Letty's mercy...'

'You said she was a pretty girl.'

'A very pretty girl,' he corrected her silkily. 'Ah, here's your father.'

Mr Crosbie joined them, very pleased with himself. Pronouncing the evening a success, he said that he had decided against asking anyone to stay on to dine and play bridge and suggested that they went at once to the dining room.

'But, Father, you planned two tables,' declared Amelia, secretly very relieved, for her bridge was beyond description, 'but you can still play—you know I'm not any good at it, and that leaves the four of you.'

Her father looked cunning. 'Ah, yes, my dear, but we're going to have a little chat after dinner.'

'All of us?'

'All of us.'

During the meal Amelia speculated as to what the little chat was going to be about. Her father was his usual jovial self, but she detected a trace of unease in his manner and Gideon, unless she was very much mistaken, was secretly amused about something. And as for her aunts, they were unable to conceal a faint, pleased excitement showing through their normal dignified manner.

She was a little surprised when her father told Badger to bring the coffee to the dining room, and when he had done so and trotted off again, she was still further surprised to find the others looking at her intently.

Her father spoke, wasting neither time nor words. 'We think you need a little change, Amelia. You've gone through a good deal just lately. . .' He coughed and looked uncomfortable. 'Gideon has most kindly brought an invitation with him that you should spend a couple of days at the New Year at his home—there's to be a family party and a few old friends; a splendid opportunity for you to meet new faces.'

Amelia looked bewildered, aware all the same of great excitement. 'But I've only got two days off. . .'

'Two days from the previous week will make four days,' pointed out Gideon matter-of-factly. 'It takes no longer for you to fly over than to drive down here. I believe you will enjoy it.'

Her two aunts nodded. It was obvious that they had been well rehearsed as a chorus. 'New friends, my dear, just what you need, and Gideon's mother there to look after you.'

Amelia blinked and wondered what tale Gideon had been telling the old ladies. She said with dignity: 'I've only just had a holiday, thank you very much just the same.'

Gideon contrived to sound authoritative, rather like the family doctor. 'Ah, yes, Amelia, but its good effects have been largely nullified by your—er—recent change of plans.'

She eyed him balefully. 'You make me sound like something from a Victorian novel!' she snapped.

He smiled lazily. 'Impossible, my dear; Victorian heroines were fair and small and drooping and very, very slender.' He added in a fair-minded manner: 'I have never called you any of those things.'

'Oh, pooh!' It was surprising to her that although she loved him so, he could annoy her to the point of throwing something at him; only her strict upbringing prevented her from doing so now. She had quite forgotten the three elderlies sitting watching them and was on the point of voicing her rage when her father said mildly: 'Now, now, Amelia, let's get back to the point. We all think a little holiday will do you good and we do all want to help you, my dear. Gideon has been most kind.'

She remembered their walk that morning then; he had indeed been kind, his gentle hands on the little frightened rabbit proved that, although looking at him now, that nasty little smile touching his firm mouth convinced her that the kindness he was showing now had no tenderness with it, a professional kindness rather, offering practical help because he saw it was needed.

She said wearily, 'Very well. I'll be delighted to accept your invitation, thank you very much.'

The words sounded empty to her ears and they must have sounded empty to Gideon's too, for the smile disappeared, leaving him looking a little stern.

'Perhaps you could fly over on Old Year's morning? Someone will meet you at Schiphol. You wouldn't need to go back until the evening of the fourth day, would you? That would give you four days. The house will be full and there will be plenty for you to do, and as your father says, a number of new faces.'

'You're very kind. It sounds fun.' Her voice held no conviction at all and the little smile reappeared.

'We'll try to make it so.'

She kept out of Gideon's way the next

morning. It wasn't until lunch time that they spoke more than a few words together and that merely concerned their return that evening to London. Lunch was a cheerful meal with a conversation which never flagged, and after the meal when they had had their coffee, dispensed by one of the aunts, Amelia offered to take one of her father's friends down to the stables to look at Trooper, the elderly horse which still worked around the grounds, while Angela remained content-edly enough with Gideon, for once losing her shyness and talking non-stop. Amelia thought their heads were very close together as she went out of the room, old Mr Bam-bridge in tow.

They left after an early dinner with Amelia making light conversation to which Gideon gave polite answer. It was only as they neared London that he observed: 'You aren't very keen on coming on a visit, are you, Amelia? But I think you may feel differently by the time you return home.'

'What do you mean?'

'Exactly what I say. Would you like to stop for a cup of coffee before we get to St Ansell's?'

She would have liked that very much; it would mean another half hour in his com-pany, but she said firmly: 'No, thanks—I've several things to do and I'm on at eight o'clock tomorrow.' She added: 'Are you going back tonight?'

'Tomorrow. I promised to look in on someone later this evening.'

Amelia almost swallowed her tongue in her efforts not to ask who the someone was. As it was she couldn't prevent herself from saying: 'I hope I haven't spoilt your evening—it's quite late.'

'Not at all. I daresay we shall go dancing.'

That beastly redhead—old what's-his-name's youngest daughter. She said, 'How nice,' in an icy voice and Gideon laughed.

'I do believe there's hope yet,' he observed.

'What for?' asked Amelia instantly.

'Who for?' he corrected her gently, and then didn't answer her question. The Victorian outlines of St Ansell's loomed out of the gloom and he turned in through the gates.

He got out of the car and opened the door for her and then walked with her to the hospital entrance, and when she would have lingered for a few minutes, loath to see him go, he cut her thanks short with a casual, 'Only too glad to give you a lift, Amelia. In any case I had to drive myself back.'

He touched her cheek briefly, his gentle finger at variance with his careless manner. 'You're too pale and you've lost weight.'

'You always say I'm fat!' A gross exaggeration which made him laugh.

'Never.' He opened the door behind her. 'Goodnight, Amelia—I'll see you on Old Year's Day. Bring some pretty dresses—there'll be at least two parties; the New Year's quite something with us, you know.'

She nodded and mumbled goodnight and hurried inside. She didn't care if she never saw him again, she told herself crossly—and at the same time felt wild with excitement at the idea of staying at his home again.

During the night she woke several times, each time more determined than ever to find some excuse for not going to Holland. She had been very silly, she decided, tossing to and fro, very wakeful. She could have avoided seeing Gideon quite easily; the less she did see of him the better; in that way she would forget him all the sooner. She slept at last and went on duty in the morning still full of her good resolutions. She told herself that she felt much better all ready and her extraordinary cheerfulness at breakfast left her friends gaping. She was just as cheerful throughout the heavy and difficult list which dragged on until the early afternoon. When it was at last at an end, she left Staff to get theatre ready for the afternoon list, mercifully a short one, and went along to her office to snatch a cup of tea and a sandwich.

There was an envelope on her desk with her name typed upon it and urgent in big letters. Amelia filled her mouth with bread and cheese and opened it. A plane ticket fell out. There was a note with it. From Gideon, it said simply: 'The plane goes at ten o'clock, don't miss it. Gideon.'

She swallowed her mouthful, drank her cooling tea, tidied herself in no time at all and rushed to the office. She had the next two days free in any case, and she had said that she would ask for two more to be added to them, but being full of high-sounding resolutions that morning she hadn't done anything about it; now probably it would be too late.

By some miracle it wasn't. The lists were so small for the days following the New Year, she could safely leave everything to Staff Nurse. Permission was granted readily and Authority even remarked that she looked a little pale and it might be wise to take a few days' holiday.

Amelia raced back upstairs, to scrub up in apparent calm while she deplored the fact that she would have no time at all to go out and buy a new dress. She would have to manage with what she had.

She chose carefully with the help and occasional hindrance of various friends. They helped her pack too and then all went down to supper, still discussing whether she had the right clothes with her, laughing a lot, careful not to mention Tom. She felt mean that although she had known most of them for years now, she didn't feel she could tell them that Tom had slipped away into a past which didn't matter any more and that she was eating her heart out for a man who treated her with the careless friendliness of someone who had known her for ever and didn't even see her. And worse, that she was fool enough to allow herself to be coerced into paying him a visit. Even with his entire family around him, she would have ample opportunity of reducing her resolutions to rubble.

CHAPTER EIGHT

AMELIA followed her fellow passengers off the plane at Schiphol in a state of panicky excitement. Supposing there was no one to meet her -- and oh, let it be Gideon she prayed silently, and don't let my insides rumble when we meet. She'd been a fool not to have eaten any breakfast and she had had only coffee on the flight; she'd been too excited for more. She went through Customs in a dream, smiling enchantingly at the serious young man who wanted to know if she had anything to declare, so that he grinned back rather sheepishly, pleased that he had someone pretty to deal with, and indeed she did look charming in the Jaeger suit and its matching top coat and little mink cap crowning her dark hair. She wished the young man a friendly goodbye and went on her way to the reception hall—packed out; no one would ever find her. Her panic returned, quite drowning the excitement for the moment as she envisaged spending hours waiting for someone to pick her up when probably she had been quite forgotten. She broke off the absurd daydream as a young man touched her arm. 'You're Miss Amelia Crosbie, are you not?'

She turned to look at him; a member of the van der Tolck family without doubt; the same handsome features and bright eyes, although not as hugely built as Gideon.

'Yes, I am. How did you know?'

He chuckled. 'Gideon told me to look for the prettiest girl on the flight. There was no mistaking you.'

She didn't much like fulsome compliments, but somehow she didn't mind him. 'Thank you, although I'm sure Gideon didn't really say anything as nice. More than likely he told you to look out for a tall well-built girl—he may even have called me fat.'

He took the case at her feet. 'I promise you he didn't. The car's outside, and I'm to drive you home; Gideon's got his hands full and the house as well. We're a large family, but I understood your family is large too.'

He was an amusing companion, telling her more about himself during the short drive than Gideon had in all the weeks she had known him. His name was Renier, he was twenty-five, just finished at the medical school at Utrecht where he had a flat of his own and was planning a trip to America. 'Just to look around, you know. I don't suppose I shall like it all that much, but Gideon says I must travel and see something of the world before I get a job.'

'What do you plan to do?' asked Amelia, much drawn to the young man.

'Oh, medicine—I'll never be as bright as Gideon, of course, but I daresay he'll take me as a partner in a few years' time.'

'You're not married or anything?'

'Lord no—we're slow starters in the family when it comes to choosing a wife. Look at old Gideon. . .' He stopped himself and added a little too quickly: 'Well, you know what I mean more than anyone else, I suppose. Here we are—there are a lot of us, but we're all nice.' He grinned at her. 'I shall call you Amelia.'

'Yes, do.' She got out of the Mercedes he had been driving and tried to make sense of his remark about Gideon - did he mean that Gideon was going to be married? Was he warning her nicely? She had no time to make up her mind: the front door was flung open and Jorrit appeared on the top step to usher them inside and almost before she had gained the hall, Gideon was coming out of a door to meet her.

His greeting was a nice mixture of casual friendliness, pleasure and gentle mockery. And why should he be smiling in that infuriatingly smug fashion? Amelia asked herself as he shook hands, there was nothing in his manner to make her think that he was anything more than just pleased to see her. His handshake had been brief as he turned his head to speak to an elderly lady coming towards them. She was of middle height, no more, comfortably plump and with a round youthful face from which sparkled a pair of very blue eyes. She was dressed in excellent taste but with no regard to fashion and her grey hair was set in an elaborate style which Amelia guessed to be several decades out of date.

'Mama —this is Amelia.' He looked down at Amelia. 'My mother.'

They shook hands under his eye before Amelia was swept away, her coat removed, into the drawing room, filled, she saw with something of dismay, with people, drinking coffee and talking at the tops of their voices.

She was given coffee in a lovely porcelain cup, offered a seat on a giant sofa between two elderly gentlemen and then introduced with smooth charm by Gideon to everyone there, and what with excitement and meeting so many strangers all at once she was soon in a fine muddle of strange-sounding names. Not that it mattered, she reminded herself; she wasn't likely to encounter any of them once she had gone away again.

She spent the next half hour or so in a whirl of small talk until presently she was led away upstairs to tidy herself for lunch. She had been given the same turret room as she had had on her previous visit and it looked delightfully welcoming with a bright fire in the old-fashioned grate and a bowl of sweet-smelling spring flowers on the dressing table. Someone had already unpacked her case and hung her clothes away, and once she had re-done her hair and face she went to the window to look out. It was a cold grey day, but there had been a heavy frost, silvery white against the sombre sky. The bare trees shuddered and swayed in the mean east wind and there wasn't a soul to see. And yet she loved it—probably, she was honest enough to admit, because Gideon lived in the middle of it all.

She was on the point of going downstairs again when there was a tap on the door and a girl of her own age came in. She said, 'Hullo,' in a friendly voice and went on, 'Gideon asked me to come up and see if you had everything you wanted. I'm his younger sister, Saskia—we did meet downstairs but you couldn't possibly remember all of us.'

She crossed the room to join Amelia at the window. 'Nice, isn't it? We—that's me and Karel and little Karel—live in Utrecht and I love it there, but I was born here and spent my life here until I married and it's like a second home, although Mama isn't here any more. She stayed a little while after Papa died, but then she went to another house we own so that Gideon's wife will feel free to do as she likes.'

So he was going to get married. Oh, well,

she'd never had any reason to think that he was even faintly interested in her —kind, yes, and fun to be with, but that was all. She would have to be careful to hide her feelings for the next day or two. Just for a moment she regretted coming but only for a moment; she would enjoy herself and treasure her visit to remember for the rest of her life. She smiled at her companion. 'It's a beautiful house,' she said seriously. 'I've just everything I could possibly need and I'm ready to go downstairs.'

Lunch was a cheerful, rather noisy meal, with Gideon at the head of the table and his mother at the foot. Amelia, sitting between Renier and a slightly older cousin, had an excellent view of them both, although she tried hard not to look at Gideon too often. All the same, she caught his eye once or more and smiled back at him wondering if the pretty brown-haired girl sitting next him on his right was the girl he was going to marry. It was a pity that she had a great many rings on both hands, and it was impossible for Amelia to see if she wore an engagement ring or not.

Everyone broke up into small groups after lunch. Some were planning a drive into Hilversum, several of the younger ones decided on a brisk walk and most of the elderlies decided comfortably to stay indoors and catch up on family news. Amelia had accepted the offer of a walk from Renier and two other girls, cousins and very much her own age. She had seen Gideon disappear into his study after lunch; presumably he had work to do and considered, quite rightly, that his guests could entertain themselves for an hour or so. She fetched her coat, wound a long scarf round her neck, pulled a woolly cap over her hair, found matching gloves, and joined the others in the hall. They were to leave by the garden door, which meant passing the study, and it was as they drew level with it that its door was flung open and Gideon, making a long arm, brought her to a halt. 'Just the girl I wanted to see,' he observed. 'You go on, all of you, we'll catch you up presently.'

He drew Amelia into the room and closed the door and she heard them clattering off laughing and talking. 'I was going for a walk,' she pointed out mildly.

'So you shall. I've something you might like to see first.'

'Oh, but I thought you were busy— working. . .'

He smiled slowly. 'Because I came here? It seemed to me to be an easy way to get you to myself without causing too much of a stir.'

She stiffened. 'Why should it cause a stir, pray?' She was suddenly cross. 'Anyway, I think I'll catch the others up. I feel like a walk.'

'I said that all wrong, didn't I? I'm sorry.' He didn't explain himself further, though, so she asked: 'What is it you wanted me to see?'

'I'll get my coat.' He led the way back through the hall and picked up a sheepskin jacket thrown down on one of the console tables. 'We might as well go through the front door,' he remarked, and glanced down at her. 'Will you be warm enough? You ought to have that padded jacket you wore in Norway.'

'That's my fishing jacket, it's years old and smells fishy.'

He tucked her hand under his arm and marched her round the side of the house towards the group of outbuildings lying in a semi-circle behind the yard. 'That was a wonderful holiday, Amelia, coming back here seemed very tame. And for you? Not a happy homecoming, was it?'

She said shortly, 'No, but I don't want to talk about it.'

He glanced at her, a thoughtful look in his eyes. 'Then we won't. This is where we get in out of the cold.' He pushed open a small door in the side of one of the barns and stood aside for her to go in too. It was warm and sweet-smelling inside, there was hay stacked against one great wall and there were two horses and a small donkey in their stalls, and in an empty stall, beyond them, was a small, silky-haired dog with a rather anxious expression and melting eyes. She whined when she saw them and then wagged her overlong tail. 'Puppies,' said Gideon, 'four of them.'

'Only a day or two old—they're sweet! I didn't see her when we were here, though.'

'She's only been here a week—I found her.' His lips tightened a little and Amelia didn't ask the question on her tongue. 'She'll join the household as soon as the puppies are safe to move, in the meantime she's happy enough here.'

'What will you do with the puppies?'

Gideon laughed. 'Mama is to have one, Saskia is to have another, and I shall keep two—the place is big enough to house five dogs.'

'Where are Nel and Prince? I haven't see them since lunch; they're always with you. . .'

'They were under my desk in the study, they know they mustn't come here just yet.'

'And who will train them? I mean, puppies need a lot of attention. . .'

He looked down at her. 'I hope my wife will take on that job.' His voice was very deliberate.

'But I didn't know that you were married. . .I mean, you weren't, were you? Have you just. . .' Her voice tailed away. Surely if he had got married his wife would be here with him, the centre of the family party?

'Oh, I'm not married yet.' He leaned down to pat the little dog, fished a biscuit from his jacket pocket and gave it to her and then handed out sugar to the donkey and horses. 'Well,' he spoke briskly, 'if we're to catch up with the others we'd better start walking.'

They went out into the cold again and she waited while he latched the door. She didn't expect his sudden hard kiss; it left her breathless and speechless and bewildered, although it didn't have that effect upon Gideon. He said in a perfectly normal voice: 'If we cut across this field, I think we'll catch them up before they get to the lake. Did they intend going on to Mayeveld, do you know?'

'I really don't know,' she told him in a high voice: her hard-won composure was in ribbons already, and she hadn't been in the house more than a few hours. She went on in a hurry: 'Does the lake freeze over if it gets really cold?'

He treated her to a detailed account of the weather conditions and their consequences. Indeed, he hadn't quite finished when they saw the others ahead of them and he let out a great shout so that they turned round and started back towards them. For all the world, thought Amelia, as though he were relieved to be shot of me. She frowned. So why did he kiss me?

A final fling before he became a married man, she supposed, walking back with one of the cousins, listening to a detailed description of the delights which lay ahead of them that evening. A lot more people after dinner, it seemed, who would dance and play round games and see the New Year in with champagne. Amelia hoped her father wouldn't be too lonely without her—although the aunts would still be there. They were on the point of entering the house when Gideon left Renier and took her arm. 'You'd like to telephone your father, wouldn't you, Amelia? Come along to the study and do it now. Later on it will be impossible—there'll be delays and you might not be able to get him at all.'

So she went back to the study with him, and this time the dogs came to greet them and then lay down again when Gideon sat down at his desk and picked up the phone. Amelia pulled off her cap and scarf and gloves and undid her coat, and presently Gideon held the phone out to her. 'Badger's gone to fetch your father,' he said, and got up to go.

Her father was pleased to hear her. 'Having a splendid time I daresay,' he declared. 'Is Gideon there?'

She said he wasn't. 'If there's a message. . .?'

'No, no—just to wish him all the best for

the New Year, and you too, my dear. We've a few friends here; dinner, you know, and a toast to the New Year, nothing as splendid as your evening will be. Have fun, my dear.'

She assured him that she would and replaced the receiver. There wasn't going to be much fun watching Gideon with his future wife, for most certainly she would be there. She gathered up her things and went upstairs, making up her mind as she went that she wouldn't look at him for the whole of the evening. There were plenty of rather nice men around, there was no reason why she shouldn't have a whale of a time. There would be champagne too, that always made her feel good.

She found herself next to Mevrouw van der Tolck at tea, being gently prodded into giving details of her work and home, and very shortly they were joined by Saskia, which made it easy for Amelia to concentrate on her two companions and ignore Gideon, wandering round the room, his tea-cup in his hand, talking to everyone. Even when he fetched up with a group of men standing close by and stayed some time with them, she managed not to look at him although her ears were stretched to hear his voice, although that was a waste of time, for he was speaking Dutch. True, he did join them presently, but only for a short time while he discussed the evening ahead with his mother, addressed a few remarks to herself, exchanged a spirited argument with his sister and strolled away again.

Amelia dressed with great care; the navy sequins, while not absolutely new, was decidedly fashionable and she would need the pleated crêpe for the following evening. She rolled her hair into an elegant chignon, stuck a sequined bow in it, and went downstairs, guided by the hum of voices and a lot of laughing.

She had hesitated about going down because she was scared to be alone with Gideon, but now she saw that the room was full; she must be the last one. She went a little pink with embarrassment and sidled round the door, making for a group of people close by. But Gideon had seen her. Before she was half way there, he was beside her, heading her off to a quiet corner, where he gave her a drink.

'You ought to have made an entrance in that dress,' he told her with a smile, 'instead of which you crept round the corner like a child late for school. Were you hoping to escape unnoticed, Amelia?'

She was regaining her cool. 'Certainly not, but I realised that I was late and the last one in always feels awful——it's like being the first one in, only that's worse.'

'Well, it wouldn't have been; we could have kept each other company and reminisced. But perhaps you don't want to do that.'

She heard the faint mockery in his voice and said uncomfortably: 'I—I don't mind.' She put down her glass and raised her lovely eyes to his face. 'Gideon, why did you ask me to come?'

'I was hoping you'd ask me that; what a pity that you did so now and here, with the entire family pretending not to look at us. Some time, when we're alone, I'll tell you. Have another drink?'

'No, thank you.' She spoke worriedly; the evening was starting all wrong. She had planned to spend the evening with anyone but him, and here she was, within seconds of entering the room, pinned into a corner with him.

'Now, I warn you that we get increasingly merry as the Old Year slips away and we bring the New Year in with something of a bang—and I mean that. Fireworks are all part and parcel of the evening.' He took her arm and walked her across to a group of young men and women - cousins, she remembered.

'Pieter's taking you into dinner.' Gideon nodded at a fair-haired youngish man in a frilled shirt and velvet jacket. Amelia took exception to them both and she wasn't sure if she liked their wearer, but he welcomed her warmly, drew her into the circle and soon she was laughing with the rest of them.

The dinner was magnificent, with silver

and crystal gleaming on white damask and
bowls of violets down the centre of the table.
Amelia ate her way through caviar, stuffed
aubergine, roast goose with all its proper
accompaniments, and a trifle as light as
thistledown, laced liberally with sherry. They
had drunk champagne and she rose from the
table decidedly improved in her spirits and
prepared to enjoy the rest of the evening to
its fullest extent.

There was no denying that it was made
easy for her to do just that. After dinner the
company moved back to the drawing room,
where they were very shortly joined by
neighbouring friends, all intent on welcoming the New Year in the proper spirit. The
silky rugs had been taken up while they were
at dinner, and Amelia found herself dancing
the moment she set foot inside the door—
with Renier and Pieter and a succession of
young men, all bent on entertaining her, but
not with Gideon. She watched him dancing
with his mother, his sisters, untold cousins
and pretty girls whom she viewed with jeal-
ous eye, but somehow he never got around
to her, not until it was almost midnight, when
he joined the little group round her, saying
smoothly: 'Our dance, I think, Amelia,' and
then sweeping her off before she could tell
him that it wasn't.

Not that she wanted to do that. Her feet
on a cloud, she spent the first few moments

listening to common sense warning her not to get excited- -after all, he must have danced with every woman in the room and it just happened to be her turn. She damped down the excitement by earnest efforts to make light, witty conversation which Gideon listened to gravely and silently, which gave her no encouragement at all.

She had lapsed into silence for perhaps ten seconds when she saw Jorrit threading his sombre way through the guests. She couldn't hear what he whispered into Gideon's ear, of course, but she saw Gideon's quick frown and was quite prepared when he said: 'Amelia, I have to go—only for a few moments —something telephoned through from the hospital.'

He walked her to a sofa where his mother was sitting, murmured a few words to that lady, and went quickly from the room. Mevrouw van der Tolck muttered something under her breath and smiled at Amelia. 'The hospital—it interferes so much with Gideon's life. Just as he had planned everything so well, too.'

'Indeed?' Amelia was all agog to hear about his plans. Possibly when she did she would be sorry, but all these rumours about his getting married. . .she had no chance, she saw that now; she should have snapped him up when he had asked her to marry him on her first visit—it had been a joke, of that she was sure, but what would he have done if she had accepted him out of hand? Besides, she hadn't been in love with him then, which made everything so much more complicated, and now the boot was on the other foot. He had been at great pains to let her see that he regarded her in the light of a good friend's daughter. Oh well. . . She was roused from her thoughts by the sudden clamour of sound and she was pulled to her feet by Renier. 'Quickly!' he told her. 'We must form a circle for Auld Lang Syne.'

'Here?' she asked him. 'Do you sing that here too?'

'Naturally, and then a great many Dutch songs.'

'Gideon's not here,' she protested.

'He will be, even if he has to bring the telephone with him.'

She was standing between Renier and one of Gideon's brothers-in-law, belting out Auld Lang Syne, when she saw Gideon come through the door at the farther end of the room. The clock began to strike midnight as he reached the circle and slid between two girls. She didn't think that he had even noticed where she was— and why should he anyway? There was a ringing cheer at the last stroke of the hour and Amelia allowed herself to be kissed unendingly while she toasted the New Year in Gideon's excellent champagne. Someone was throwing streamers and balloons, discreetly launched by a severe-looking Jorrit, were being tossed around. Amelia had just fielded one neatly back to an elderly bearded gentlemen whom she remembered vaguely as an uncle of some importance in the family when she was taken hold of firmly and whisked through the celebrations, out of a side door and into a small room she had never seen before.

'A happy new year, Amelia,' said Gideon softly. 'Happier, I hope, than the last one. Personally, I have no complaints to make on that score—the Old Year has given me some very pleasant memories.'

'Oh, has it?' She had gone a little way away from him, to stand by a small bureau whose marquetry lid she was tracing with a forefinger.

'Indeed yes. One waits, you know, for something for a long time, knowing that if one waits long enough it will happen, and it has.'

'Oh, good. Did you discover a new anaesthetic or something?'

'I discovered the girl I intend to marry.'

'Do I know her?' She made the question an airy one.

'Yes.'

It would be that beastly Fiona. 'She was at Barbara's wedding?'

'Yes.'

'Then why isn't she here?' she asked

sharply. 'You shouldn't have let her go off to America like that.'

She was still so intent on the bureau that she didn't see his eyes widen with surprise and then narrow with amusement. He said to ruffle her false calm: 'Have you heard from Tom?'

She shook her head. 'No, but I didn't expect to.'

'I'm a little surprised; I should have thought that once he was out there and had had a look around, he would have had second thoughts.'

Amelia turned on him fiercely. 'Look, I'm not going to be any man's second thought,' but she was not thinking of Tom at all, only of Gideon, amusing himself with her while his Fiona was safely in America.

Gideon's face had become all at once bland. 'You feel very strongly about that, don't you, Amelia?' He smiled slowly at her. 'How serious we have become—and in the middle of a party too! Shall we go back and see how everyone is getting on?'

She said yes with such alacrity that her tongue tripped over the word. She would have liked to have left the party and gone to her room and howled and howled until she had no tears left, instead of which she would have to dance and laugh and chatter for hours yet.

Something which she achieved very

creditably until the party broke up shortly before three o'clock, by which time she was so tired she had no wish to think about anything at all, certainly not her own unhappiness.

She was on her way up to bed, mounting the staircase beside Mevrouw van der Tolck, when Gideon called her softly from the hall below. She paused to look down at him almost cross-eyed with sleep.

'Come down, Amelia, just for a moment.'

There was no reason why she should retrace her steps so obediently, but she did. The hall was dimly lit now and Mevrouw van der Tolck didn't look round as she reached the head of the staircase and started along the gallery to her room. Amelia could hear Jorrit talking to someone behind the closed doors of the drawing room and the heavy breathing of Nel and Prince waiting to be taken for a last run before their master went to his bed, she was conscious of the heavy tick-tock of the great Friesian wall clock too, but these small sounds only served to make the silence of the old house deeper. She crossed the hall to where Gideon stood and fetched up before him.

'Well?' she asked.

He didn't answer her, only took her in his arms and kissed her gently.

'A farewell to the Old Year,' he explained, 'but I don't think we'll do anything about the

New Year at the moment—I like to be sure of my facts.'

Amelia looked up at him, owl-like. 'I haven't the faintest idea what you mean,' she told him with something of a snap. Her misery, dulled by tiredness, had returned even more sharply because he'd kissed her.

'No, I'm sure you don't.' He was staring down at her, his arms still around her despite the surreptitious tug with which she had tried to free herself. 'You're in a muddle, aren't you, Amelia? Your pretty head is filled with fancies and quite absurd notions and you've got to get rid of them.'

She pulled away from him then and turned her back, her eyes full of tears. 'Don't you preach at me,' she said in a voice becoming a little shrill. 'I'll manage my own life, thank you.'

'You see what I mean?' he asked mildly. 'That's another absurd notion.'

Amelia didn't wait for more but flew away at a great rate and up the stairs and into her room, where she burst into tears, something she had been wanting to do for at least five minutes. Everything was so hopeless! If only he hadn't been going to marry Fiona she might have told him everything—that she didn't love Tom, that she loved him. She might even have asked him humbly if he had meant it when he had asked her to marry him, because if he did, she would, very willingly—that Tom had never meant the same to her as he did, that without him life was going to be bleak. . .and thank God I didn't say all that, wailed Amelia between hic-coughs.

She dried her eyes presently and went to bed where naturally enough she fell asleep at once, quite worn out with despair and tiredness. She didn't wake until she was roused by her early morning tea, only by then it wasn't early at all, but well past nine o'clock. She got up at once and went down-stairs to find most of the younger members of the party at the breakfast table, and she was immediately drawn into a discussion about the night's festivities, pronounced great fun by everyone there. 'Such a pity that Gideon had to leave so early,' observed Saskia.

Amelia buttered toast with a hand which shook. 'Oh, did he? But we didn't go to bed until three o'clock.'

'He didn't go to bed at all—saw us all safely upstairs, then takes the dogs out and races off to Utrecht for some dire emergency or other.' Saskia peered into her coffee cup. 'He needs a wife to keep an eye on him — don't you agree, Amelia?'

Amelia kept her eyes on her plate. 'Yes, oh, yes, I'm sure he does.'

A cousin from the other end of the table joined in: 'I pity the poor girl—keeping an eye on him will be a round-the-clock job.'

'Well, that wouldn't be much of a hardship.' It was his second sister, Chloe, speaking. 'Gideon's a darling. A good thing he's made up his mind at last.'

There was a profound silence, and Amelia, her eyes still on her plate, didn't see the eyes of the van der Tolck family fastened apprehensively upon her. Chloe had always been too quick with her tongue, as everyone was quick enough to tell her later. Now she made amends as speedily as possible by demanding to know rather loudly what they were all going to do.

'I shall take Amelia down to the stables to see that dear little dog Gideon found,' observed Saskia, 'and there are crowds of people coming to lunch, don't forget. Gideon'll be home by then.'

'Won't he want to sleep for a little?' ventured Amelia. Poor Gideon, not getting to bed at all, and she had been so ungracious, though possibly he had forgotten all about it. . . . His mind would be wholly occupied by Fiona.

'If I know him, he'll have a shower, change his clothes, snore his head off for ten minutes and be the life and soul of the party.' Renier smiled across the table at Amelia. 'You must find us a very peculiar family.'

She shook her head, wishing with all her heart that she could become a member of it.

Probably Renier had been right about

Gideon, for when lunch time came, there he was, being the perfect host, the picture of a leisurely man with nothing much to do. Only when she looked carefully at him when he couldn't see her doing it did she see the lines etched between nose and mouth and the marked droop of his eyelids. He looked up and saw her and she turned her back quickly and began talking to a tall, very thin young man who she felt sure was about to tell her his life's history.

Gideon's voice in her ear prevented that. 'Your face was a mixture of pity and surprise and something else— why?'

She wasn't going to be caught out. 'Well, that's easy—I was feeling sorry because you had no sleep last night, and surprise that you're here, looking so—so. . .'

'Alert? happy? handsome? You choose. What was the other look, Amelia?'

'I have no idea.' She gave him what she hoped was a cool smile and turned back to the thin young man. He had gone. 'I was talking to someone,' she protested.

'Cousin Theodore—twenty-one, garrulous and full of conceit. I'm much more interesting.' She giggled and he said: 'That's better. Don't you find me interesting?'

Amelia twiddled her glass round and round in her hand until he took it away from her and put it on a table. 'I thought we might go for a long walk after lunch.'

'Don't you need some sleep?'

'I can sleep later. I thought we might go round the park and down to the village—the church is rather special.'

'Well, yes—all right. Just us?'

His raised eyebrows sent the colour into her cheeks. 'I am considered to be a very safe companion even for the prettiest of young women.'

'I'm sorry—I didn't mean that.' It was annoying of him to ask at once:

'Then what did you mean?'

'Oh, nothing—I was just saying anything to—to keep the conversation going.'

'Oh, dear, am I such hard work?' He was laughing at her now and she said crossly:

'You know I didn't mean that.' She was about to try and explain in a light and joking fashion when they were joined by several others and presently Gideon moved away. Probably, Amelia told herself unhappily, he won't want to take me for a walk now.

It seemed that he did. She had barely finished her coffee when he asked her if she would like to get her coat. 'For it gets dark early,' he explained, and, 'Do put on something warm, it's a good deal colder.'

It was indeed very cold. She wore her thick topcoat and borrowed a fur hood belonging to someone or other and dug her hands into thick mitts. But ten minutes' brisk walking set her glowing so that her cheeks were red and her eyes sparkling. 'Gosh, it's frosty,' she remarked as they skirted the field beyond the stables.

Gideon threw her a sidelong glance. 'Yes, it is. And I see no sign of a thaw.'

She looked around her. 'No, but it's lovely just the same.'

'I'm waiting for the silver thaw, Amelia.'

She knew what he meant and she wasn't a girl to evade the issue. 'Well, there isn't going to be one,' she told him flatly, 'and I can't think why you keep on about it.'

'I should like to see you happy, Amelia.'

She slipped on a patch of ice and he flung an arm around her and kept it there. 'Just because you're so happy yourself,' she said slowly, 'it doesn't mean that you have to see that everyone else is happy.'

'Not everyone, just you.' He lifted her neatly over a tree trunk fallen in their path. 'Why don't you write to Tom? You know, when you're in love you shouldn't give up so easily.'

'I don't want to talk about it,' she told him in a mulish voice, 'it'll spoil the walk.'

'In that case let us concentrate on the scene around us.' His voice was light as though he were glad to change the subject. 'There's the village beyond the line of trees, it's still light enough to see round the church; we can go back along the road.'

The church was charming; much too large

for the village, towering over the small houses crowded round it, its plain glass windows rather austere, its doors tight shut until someone who had seen them pass came running with a key to open a side door.

The interior was lofty and very cold, its white-washed walls reflecting the winter sky outside. The pulpit with its enormous sounding-board dominated the old-fashioned pews beneath it, and the walls were half covered by plaques of the long departed, most of them, Amelia saw, van der Tolcks.

'Has your family lived here for a long time?' she asked, frowning over an imposs-ible-to-understand inscription held by a well built angel.

'Oh, lord yes—the castle was built in the fourteenth century.'

'And you've—your family—have lived there ever since?'

'Yes, always a direct line of succession, too.' Gideon smiled briefly. 'We've always gone in for a lot of children.'

It reminded her of his remarks about his children having a lovely home in which to grow up. She turned her back on the angel and concentrated on a funeral urn upheld by a female heavily draped and veiled.

'I've been waiting,' observed Gideon blandly, 'for you to ask me whom I intend to marry.'

'Well, I'm not going to—I don't want to

know.' She paused. 'At least, I can guess, but I still don't want to know. Not ever.' She drew a deep breath. 'Please, Gideon, don't talk about it.'

'Just as you wish. Do come and look at this marble group—a very ancient ancestor of mine, with his wife—aren't the children delightful? Six boys on one side and six girls on the other.'

And after that he led her round the church, showing her everything, answering her questions in a tolerant, goodhumoured manner which made her feel as though she were a stranger being given a conducted tour by a guide. And later, as they walked back, he kept up a steady flow of casual talk, the kind of talk with which a good host would indulge a not very well-known guest. Amelia supposed she had deserved it.

There were more people to dinner that evening but no dancing afterwards, just gossip and a good deal of laughter. Amelia, in the claret crêpe-de-chine, would have enjoyed it all very much if only Gideon had made an effort to talk to her over and above the polite enquiries as to whether she would like another drink or was she warm enough, and what pleasure she did have was rendered quite hollow by overhearing him telling one of the English guests present that he had just received a telephone call from America. So that when, towards the end of the evening, he came and sat down beside her with the air of a man who intended to settle for some time, she said yes and no and oh, really and nothing else—and then, being female to her very bones, was furious with him when on the slightest of excuses, he went away again.

She allowed herself a good burst of tears when she was in bed and relieved her feelings by calling Fiona all the names under the sun.

She was leaving after lunch the next day and Renier had told her that he would drive her to Schiphol, and since Gideon hadn't even hinted that he would be seeing her off himself—and indeed why should he?—she had accepted gladly. She took an affectionate leave of his mother and brothers and sisters and since Gideon had been absent for the whole morning, left polite messages for him and went out to the car with Renier. She was replying suitably to Jorrit's gravely spoken farewell when she saw the Rolls coming very fast round the curve of the drive. It stopped beside Renier's car and Gideon got out and walked unhurriedly up the steps, saying something to Renier as he came. 'Beautifully timed,' he observed to Amelia's astonished face. 'I wasn't relishing the prospect of chasing you all the way to Schiphol.'

'But Renier's taking me. . .'

'I'm taking you—he was the stand-in in case I couldn't make it.'

She could think of nothing to say. She sat

beside him, quite silent, wishing she had the nerve to say all the things she wanted to and knowing that she wouldn't. Gideon didn't say anything either but occupied himself with driving, occasionally whistling softly to himself, which Amelia found very irritating to her already stretched nerves.

They were actually at Schiphol and she was nicely embarked on her farewell speech when he cut her short. 'Let's not waste time, we've done that too often already, and now, damn it, we've only a couple of minutes when we could have talked while we drove.' He bent to look into her face. 'You see, my dear, you're still frosted over, aren't you?' He kissed her suddenly and quite roughly. 'And if it's of any interest to you, Amelia, Fiona isn't the girl I've set my heart on.'

A well-modulated voice from somewhere in the roof begged those for the London flight to get a move on. 'I'm coming to see you,' said Gideon, and kissed her again before giving her a gentle push through the gateway to her plane.

CHAPTER NINE

AMELIA flung herself into her work with a vigour to cause her nurses to raise eyebrows behind her back and exchange significant glances when they thought she wasn't looking. The lists weren't heavy and she embarked on a campaign of cleaning, repairing and replacing which left everyone breathless and the various departments decidedly edgy. She might have gone on for days like this, snappy with her friends, austerely civil with everyone else, if there hadn't been a bad accident close to the hospital in the early hours of the morning. It had been a cold night, icy underfoot, and now just after dawn and foggy, a crowded bus had had no chance when it was rammed by a van loaded with furniture.

Amelia, called urgently to go to the theatre at once, dressed fast, bundled her hair up, fastened it ruthlessly with pins thrust in at random and rushed through the hospital. Even her early morning face, devoid of make-up, looked beautiful in the bleak lights of the passages she hurried through. Almost there, she met the RSO and they both stopped to exchange vital information. 'A bus,' he told her, enlarging on the information she had had from the nurse who had called her. 'Packed—they're still getting them out. Get both theatres going, will you? We'll do the small stuff in the Accident Room, but there are bound to be urgent cases for you.' He eyed her carefully. 'You're very untidy.'

Amelia had never liked him overmuch; he was a good surgeon and reliable, but he lacked a sense of humour, but all she said mildly was: 'Yes, aren't I? I didn't waste much time dressing, but I'm here and in my right mind. Give me as much warning as you can, won't you?'

She tore on, upstairs and through the swing doors and straight into her office, where she lifted the receiver and dialled the Accident Room.

'Janet? Amelia here. Look, let me have some idea of what to expect as soon as you know, will you? I met Mr Lord on the way here, but he'll probably forget. . .'

'OK. It's pretty grim—we're in for a busy day. I'll give you a ring just as soon as I know something.'

The first case came up ten minutes later, a young man with a fractured base of skull. Amelia scrubbed for him, sending Sybil to the second theatre to do the same for a young woman with severe lacerations. And after that they kept on coming, between them they managed to snatch a mug of tea, but that was all; breakfast was out of the question, there weren't enough of them to spare even one at a time. They were on their third case when Doctor Gough, the senior anaesthetist, gave up his stool with a thankful: 'I'll be back in fifteen minutes. Will you be going back to the Accident Room?'

Amelia, bent over her trolley, dropped the forceps in her hand at Gideon's quiet voice. 'Thomley-Jones asked me to stay up here for a while, to take over from Owen in the other theatre—he's been up for most of the night, I understand.'

She signed to a nurse to pick up the forceps, finished the exact arrangement of the instruments and gently kicked the trolley into position with one foot. Only then did she glance to the head of the table where Gideon was sitting over his patient, very large and anonymous in his gown and cap. He didn't look at her, though, which was just as well, for her heart was hammering against her ribs, sounding loud in her ears, so that she glanced around to see if anyone had heard it too. Apparently not. The RSO, who had relieved Mr Thomley-Jones for that case, requested towel clips and forceps, and she began once more on her well-learned duties, her mind empty now but for the task in hand.

The operation took a long time. The elderly patient was covered with small deep wounds caused by glass, each one of which had to be explored and then stitched, and all the while Gideon didn't look at her—perhaps he didn't know she was there, she allowed herself the fleeting thought as she began clearing for the next case while the RSO attended to the very last cut.

Two student nurses and a part-time staff nurse reported for duty as the patient was wheeled away, and Amelia was able to send her own nurse down to a meal. The staff nurse wasn't too happy about taking cases, but Amelia assured her that there was nothing to it, and sent Sybil to a meal too. She was getting the next trolley ready when Sybil poked her head round the door.

'Look, Sister, let me take over here while you have something. . .'

Amelia went to the sink to scrub up. 'Thanks a lot, but I think that if Staff Wilkes takes your next case—it's only a flesh wound of the leg and pretty straightforward--you can come back here and take over from me. There's a ruptured spleen coming up now; by the time that's done you'll be back. Is Wilkes able to cope, do you think?'

'She'll have to.'

Amelia nodded. 'Take Nurse Carter with you, one of the relief nurses can take over from her—I'd better have the other one in here.'

'Right, Sister.' Sybil's head disappeared

and then reappeared. 'I say, who's the giant in the anaesthetic room?'

'He's just popped in to give a hand. Sybil, find out how they're getting on in the AR, will you?'

'OK. Shall I ask them to send some food to the office for you?'

'That's an idea. Ask Gertie to make some tea and boil me an egg or something, but not until this case is finished.'

Sybil's head disappeared again and Amelia, tied into her sterile gown, put on her gloves and bent to her trolleys, ticking off in her tired head all the things that should be upon them. She was testing a Moynihan's clamp when Gideon walked in. His 'Hullo', was friendly and calm and he went on just as calmly: 'If you've nothing better to do this evening I should like to give you dinner.'

She had gone very pink, thankful that nothing of her face was visible behind the mask. 'I can think of absolutely nothing better to do than eat at the moment,' she told him. 'By this evening I shall be famished— you'll have to bear with me making a pig of myself.'

'I think we know each other well enough for that.' His voice was bland.

Dick Dive, one of the house surgeons, put his head round the door: 'The next one's ready, sir,' and Gideon went away, leaving Amelia feeling a bit overawed because Dick had called him 'sir' so respectfully, and to wonder how and why he was there, anyway.

She asked him that much later, at the end of a long day's work, when bathed and dressed in a deep pink silk jersey dress, her tired face nicely made up, she sat opposite Gideon in the upstairs room at the White Tower. She had eaten a splendid meal; taramosalata, kebab de turbota la polita, and a lovely rich honey-and-pastry pudding loaded with calories. Now, over coffee, she sighed deeply with satisfaction, filled their cups and asked: 'Why are you in England?' and when he didn't answer at once: 'I didn't know you knew Mr Thomley-Jones. . .'

'An old friend, as it happens. I came to see you, Amelia.'

Her heart gave a great thump under her ribs. 'Oh, why?'

His face was as bland as his voice. 'To see if you were happy in your work.'

She said, too sharply: 'Of course I'm happy   I don't have time for half the things I want to do. . .'

He said evenly: 'In that case I won't waste any of it asking you to marry me. And talking of time, without in any way wishing to bring this pleasant little meeting to a close, should you be going back? It's almost midnight, and I saw tomorrow's list.'

Amelia was speechless with rage and humiliation and misery, but she fixed some sort of a smile on to her shaking mouth and rose to leave at once. Only minutes later, as she sat beside him in the car, she voiced the thought uppermost in her mind. 'But you're going to marry Fiona.'

She had left it too late, of course. He turned into the hospital's forecourt and stopped outside the entrance and before he answered her he got out, opened her door and walked the few paces to the door. 'You are a very silly girl, Amelia,' he told her, 'and your head is a jumble of rubbish which you have stored away with no thought as to its accuracy. And you are still frostbound.'

He pushed the door open and, unable to think of a word to say, Amelia went through it.

The morning's list was indeed a heavy one, and made worse because she hadn't slept at all, and even more shattering was the fact that despite that, she hadn't the faintest idea what she was going to do. Strong tea at breakfast helped a little, and so did two hours' steady work with no chance to think about herself. It was during the third case, a myotomy, that she knew what she was going to do. She would be off at five o'clock, she would find Gideon and tell him that she loved him and did he really want to marry her. She'd wanted to do that, but somehow she had never had the chance —now she would make one. And he wouldn't be hard to find.

She had heard Mr Thomley-Jones invite him to dinner; he hadn't mentioned a date, but he had said in a couple of days' time, which meant that Gideon was staying in London. He might even be at the hospital at that very moment. Life all at once became a lot easier. True, her world might still collapse in ruins around her feet, but at least she would know. . .

The RSO was stitching up and Mr Thomley-Jones was stripping off his gloves when she heard him say casually: 'Van der Tolck should be back home by now. A pity, there was that case I wanted to see him about. . .' He went off muttering to himself and Amelia, tidying up after him, thought numbly that it served her right. She should have spoken up when she'd been with Gideon on the previous evening. Even if he'd been joking. . . Suddenly she knew that she wasn't going on like that for a moment longer. She pushed the trolley away from her, caught Sybil's eye and asked her to take over. 'It's still ten minutes to dinner time, but I'm going early. There's only that lipoma and Mr Lord will do it.'

Amelia didn't stop for more. With her purse in her hand, she started for the lift, thanking God as she went that it happened to be her turn for early dinner. The lift stopped to allow a wheelchair and its occupant to be loaded in, but the porter was slow and after a few impatient moments she squeezed past and took to the stairs.

The telephone box in the hall had someone in it and there were two people waiting. Amelia didn't waste time but ran out of the door and across the forecourt and into the street, packed with lunch time crowds. There were telephone boxes, four of them, only a hundred yards away.

Gideon, in the porter's lodge, waiting with some impatience for the man on duty to ring theatre, watched with astonishment tinged with amusement as Amelia swept past into the dreary chill outside. He bade the man leave it and started unhurriedly after her. His Amelia had looked distraught and, he had to admit, very cross. It would be as well to see where she was going.

Amelia beat a stout lady with an umbrella by a few seconds to the end telephone box and shut the door on her frustrated face before putting through her call to Holland. At least she knew Gideon's number, and she got it surprisingly quickly. It was Jorrit who answered and, taking a deep breath, she asked for Gideon, only to be told he wasn't there.

'Not there?' she repeated like an idiot. 'But he must be—they said. . .I must speak to him!'

She was aware that the door had been opened behind her and she turned round, ready to argue with the woman, only it was

Gideon standing there, filling the doorway and quite half of the phone box, so that she found her nose pressed to his waistcoat. She was in quite a state by now, two angry tears trickled down her cheeks and she was having trouble with her breathing. She let the receiver dangle by its cord. 'I'm ringing you and you're not there!' she told him furiously.

Gideon picked up the receiver, spoke into it, replaced it on its hook and because it made more room, put an arm round her. 'What did you want to tell me?' he asked.

'You'd gone,' she muttered into his chest. 'They said you'd gone home and I—I couldn't bear it. I wanted to tell you that I loved you, only each time I tried you were so casual and—and friendly, but now I don't care what you are, you can laugh if you want to, only if you don't love me, just say so and go away!' She beat his shoulder with a furious fist; it was like hitting a tree trunk and just as painful.

Gideon smiled down at her tenderly. 'The silver thaw at last,' he said softly, and kissed her with leisurely satisfaction, 'and I must say it suits you: all these weeks I've been waiting—ever since the moment I saw you, my darling heart, and now—now it's like standing in the countryside, watching the sun turn the frost to silver as it thaws.' He studied her flushed tearful face. 'It's better than that,' he added, and kissed her again, interrupted this time by the woman with the umbrella who had managed to open the door a little wider behind him and poke him on the shoulder. 'I never did, young man!' she exclaimed furiously.

Gideon looked over his shoulder at her. 'Then, my dear madam, may I suggest that you do as soon as possible? It's most enjoyable.'

The woman retreated looking stunned and he finished the interrupted kiss. They might have been on a desert island, or for that matter sitting on top of the world.

Amelia kissed him back. 'Oh, dear Gideon, what shall we do?'

He drew her out on to the pavement, where they stood, delighted with each other's company, while the unseeing crowd pushed and jostled past them.

'Why, get married, my darling.' Gideon looked around him. 'It's your lunch hour, isn't it? There's something called Percy's Place across the street, we'll get a cup of tea and a sandwich and talk about it, shall we?'

'Oh, Gideon, please — there's such a lot to say. . .'

She was interrupted by the woman with the umbrella who suddenly thrust her face between them.

'Well, congrats, I'm sure,' she shouted, and nodded her head in its deplorable hat.

She smiled unexpectedly. 'Go on, give 'er another kiss!'

And Gideon did.

MILLS & BOON

BETTY NEELS

COLLECTOR'S EDITION

If you have missed any of the previously published titles in the Betty Neels Collector's Edition, you may order them by sending a cheque or postal order (please do not send cash) made payable to Harlequin Mills & Boon Ltd. for £2.99 per book plus 50p postage and packing for the first book and 25p for each additional book. Please send your order to: Betty Neels Collector's Edition, P.O. Box 236, Croydon, Surrey, CR9 3RU (EIRE: Betty Neels Collector's Edition, P. O. Box 4546, Dublin 24).